Anneke Jans *in the* New World

Anneke Jans in the New World

A Novel

SANDRA FREELS

SHE WRITES PRESS

Published in 2026 by
She Writes Press, an imprint of The Stable Book Group

32 Court Street, Suite 2109
Brooklyn, NY 11201
https://shewritespress.com

Library of Congress Control Number: 2025917865
ISBN: 979-8-89636-032-2
eISBN: 979-8-89636-033-9

Interior designer: Katherine Lloyd, The DESK

Printed in the United States

For Sarah, Jessy, and Sam

TABLE OF CONTENTS

AUTHOR'S NOTE

Anneke Jans in the New World is a fictional biography of a real woman who immigrated from Europe to North America nearly four hundred years ago. At the time of her journey, the Dutch Republic had awarded a contract to the Dutch West India Company (WIC) to exploit the resources of that part of North America they called New Netherland. The WIC was primarily interested in the fur trade, but in time the impulse toward colonization triumphed, which led to a remarkably diverse society. New Netherland was certainly multilingual and multiethnic. The "Dutch" included French, German, and Scandinavians, as well as transplants from Southern and Eastern Europe. The Dutch Reformed Church was the only denomination permitted to openly practice, but freedom of conscience was the law of the land, with the result that members of other religious groups were free to worship in private as they saw fit.

European immigrants who made their homes in New Netherland interacted with American Indians speaking various Algonquian dialects, including Munsee and Mohican, and with the Iroquoian-speaking Mohawks. Although the court records of the colony, made available online by the New Netherland Institute, often refer to individual tribes and their leaders by name, Indians in general were more commonly called *Wilden*. This term, which derives from the word "wild," is sometimes translated as "savages," but it also has the connotation of "native to this place," which is in part why I have chosen to retain it in this novel. I have also included a few words of Lenape taken from *The Lenape Talking Dictionary*, although I know modern Lenape is bound to be very different from the languages spoken in New Netherland four centuries ago.

European newcomers also interacted with Africans. In 1627, a group of at least eleven enslaved Africans, most likely taken from a Portuguese prize ship, were brought to New Amsterdam. Slavery was prohibited in the Dutch Republic, and initially in the colony there seemed to be some confusion between indentured servitude and slavery. The original cohort of slaves were allowed many of the same legal rights and privileges as the colonists, including the right to marry and raise families and the right to have their complaints adjudicated in court. In 1644, this group petitioned for freedom, and their petition was granted. In the meanwhile, however, the WIC had entered the slave trade, which resulted in the commodification of Africans and increased codification and severity of rules and regulations governing their lives. This book's protagonist, Anneke Jans, knew enslaved Africans and almost certainly benefited from their labor, but she herself was never an enslaver.

Anneke Jans in the New World is an act of imagination, but Anneke Jans (1605–1663) was a real person who lived in a complex society on the cusp of our own modern world. In telling her story, I have tried to stay as close as possible to the known facts of her life, but where the record is unclear, I have written this novel in a way that I believe is true to its era. I wish to acknowledge the harm done to American Indians and to enslaved Africans and their descendants during the American colonial period, and I have also tried to imagine what it felt like to live within that world of rapid change when motivations were unclear and outcomes uncertain. My characters witness and sometimes perpetrate acts of brutality, and they sometimes express themselves in the prejudicial language of fear and ignorance. This story could have been told in many different ways, but my intention has been to express it in one of the ways it really could have happened.

A NOTE ON NAMES

People

Anneke Jans in the New World is a fictionalized account of events that took place in the Dutch colony of New Netherland in the seventeenth century. The names of most of the characters appear in the historical documents of the period. Many of those characters use patronymics, a form of their father's name that means "son of" or "daughter of," rather than surnames. Anneke Jans, for example, is Anna daughter of Jan, but her oldest daughter is Sara Roelofs, Sara daughter of Roelof, and her oldest son is Jan Roelofsen, Jan son of Roelof.

Women are most often referred to by diminutives of their given names, so Anna Jans is known as Anneke ("Annie"), and her sister Maria Jans is Marritje ("Molly").

Places

The colony of New Netherland included parts of what are now New York, New Jersey, Pennsylvania, Maryland,

Connecticut, and Delaware. The most important place names in the novel are:

- New Amsterdam—the chief settlement, today's lower Manhattan
- North River—today's Hudson River
- Rensselaerswyck—the area surrounding today's Albany, New York
- Fort Orange and Beverwyck—today's Albany, New York
- Esopus and Wiltwyck—today's Kingston, New York

One

ARRIVAL

(1630)

New Amsterdam

When the *Eendracht* dropped anchor off the tip of Manhattan Island, Anneke should have been relieved that their long voyage was nearly over, but instead she stood by the railing of the ship, tightly gripping Roelof's hand. Accustomed to the flat gray horizon of the Dutch polders, she found the spring sunlight sparkling off the pristine waters of the harbor unnerving, and the dense forest that covered the hills rising in the distance filled her with dread.

"How will we ever live here?" she asked. "There are no people, no buildings, nothing but wild animals and savages."

"It's too late to turn back now," Roelof said. "And besides, there *are* people here. Look, there's Fort Amsterdam." He pointed to a small fortification directly ahead of them where two lounging sentries, matchlocks by their sides, stared at the newcomers. Closer to the water's edge, a larger crowd had gathered to meet the newly arrived ship.

Roelof was right, of course, but knowing that it was too late to turn back, that they had left behind forever family and friends and the only home they had ever known only intensified Anneke's fear. It was all her mother's fault. All of Amsterdam had been awash in rumors of the vast fortunes to be made by investing in the colonial ventures of the Dutch West India Company, more commonly known as the WIC. Anneke had heard the rumors, just like everybody else, but she knew those vast fortunes weren't for the likes of her and Roelof.

Her mother, Tryn Jonas, working as a dry nurse in the home of diamond merchant Kiliaen van Rensselaer, had had other ideas.

"Listen," she said to her daughters Anneke and Marritje and to son-in-law Roelof, "here's what we must do. The WIC has already sent more than one shipload of settlers to New Netherland, and there will be others. Where there are people, there will be babies. If I can get them to hire me as midwife, I can take care of myself and Marritje. Then, Heer Van Rensselaer has been granted a patroonship there. He's willing to pay the expenses of families who will work on his farmsteads. Roelof, I want you and Anneke to be one of those families." Anneke had protested, but Tryn prevailed, saying, "Anneke, a seaman's wife lives like a widow even when her man's still alive. Do this for Roelof so you can spend your time on Earth together instead of wondering whether he will ever come home again."

Anneke gripped Roelof's hand even more tightly and smiled up at him through her tears. "I don't want to turn back," she said. "I want to be with you."

For the rest of the morning, tender boats ferried passengers, livestock, cargo, and crew from the *Eendracht* to the dock. Wolfert Gerritsen, who would be the new Director of

Rensselaerswyck, shook hands with Roelof as he departed and gave Anneke a quick hug.

"I'm going to arrange to have farming equipment, livestock, and seed shipped ahead to Fort Orange. Then I'll go there directly to make sure everything's ready for your arrival. I'll see you in a month or so."

Anneke gathered up their meager possessions—clothing, bed linens, and a few cooking utensils—and packed them away in Roelof's old sea chest. *Had they brought enough?* Tryn had assured them that everything they might possibly need would be available for purchase here, but looking at the half-finished buildings that lined the quay, Anneke had her doubts. Her packing completed, she turned her attention to four-year-old Sara and two-year-old Katryn. *How in the world was she supposed to make them presentable after two months at sea?* Washing was out of the question, so at last she contented herself with wiping their faces and dressing them in the clean aprons and caps she had set aside for their arrival.

Roelof gave final instructions to Claes and Jacob, the two farm boys Tryn had recruited to join their party. "Remember," he told them, "we will not be staying long here in New Amsterdam, so don't get too comfortable. Heer Van Rensselaer expects us to proceed north as quickly as possible. It's already May, and he wants us to sow at least five morgens of wheat before the hard frosts come."

At last their turn came to disembark, and Roelof and Anneke finally set foot on the land they planned to call home. Unsteady after so many long weeks at sea, Anneke walked cautiously along the unpaved road, trying not to step in the refuse that lay all about. The girls clung to her skirt, but they were fascinated by everything they saw. Sara spotted a group of copper-colored men wearing tight leather leggings and coats made of blue duffle. Their straight black hair appeared to be long in some places and shaved in others. "Look, Mamma," she exclaimed. "Are those Wilden?"

"Hush, Daughter, it's rude to stare," Anneke said, but she herself was staring at a group of Africans who were making repairs to the fort. She had seen Africans before back in Amsterdam but never so many of them working together. Katryn had noticed a dead hog lying in the middle of the road and was trying to hold onto her mother with one hand while holding her nose with the other.

As they made their way along the waterfront, a pock-faced man with a heavy German accent called out from the door of his tavern to ask whether they needed a place to stay. "No," Roelof replied, "but can you direct us to Dirck Holgertsen's?"

"Sure I can," the taverner answered, "but that's Dirck over there." He pointed to a stocky blond man loading wares from the *Eendracht* onto a cart.

Roelof waved his thanks and then hailed the carter in Norwegian. "Hei, Dirck, I have letters for you from Tryn Jonas."

Dirck jerked his head up in surprise at being addressed in his native tongue. "Newcomers, heh? Help me get this lot delivered to the WIC warehouse, and then we'll hear what Tryn has to say."

Roelof and Claes began shifting heavy containers of axes and adzes while Jacob loaded bundles of undyed duffle. Anneke sat off to one side on their old sea chest, holding the sleeping Katryn on her lap. The quay was not crowded—at least not by Amsterdam standards—but everyone there seemed to bustle about with important business. A tall European dressed in a homemade costume of deerskin walked down the middle of the road with a bundle of beaver pelts slung over his shoulder. A group of people, both European and Wilden, were bartering for food. *Where are the shops?* she wondered. She noticed how few old people there were, none really, and how few women and children. *So,* she thought, *it's a country of young men*. She reached over and pulled Sara close. "We're on our own here, girls," she whispered. "We're going to have to make our own rules and be very quick-witted and careful if we mean to survive."

After the last load had been delivered, Dirck helped Anneke and the girls clamber into the cart, and they set off for his house on the north side of the fort. "When we get there," he cautioned them, "we will need to speak Dutch. My wife, Christine, is French, and she's never gotten her tongue around Norwegian."

"Mes cher enfants!" Christine exclaimed when she saw Sara and Katryn. She won their hearts by hustling them to the back of the house and setting them down before bowls of warm apple custard swimming in clotted cream—the first real food they had tasted since leaving Texel more than two months ago. She kissed Anneke on the cheek. "You poor thing. You must be exhausted. Sit here on your trunk and don't worry about a thing. Tomorrow we will heat a kettle and wash all of your linens, but today you must rest."

Christine bustled about setting everyone at ease. "You know," she said to Sara, "I was also a little girl when I first came here six years ago." Anneke looked at her quizzically. This tiny woman with frizzy black hair peeping out from under her cap was small enough to be a child, but clearly she was already a married woman with children of her own and another on the way.

"It's true," Christine said, turning to Anneke. "Well, I was a little older than your Sara but not by much, and my two little sisters were exactly the same ages your girls both are now. My father, God rest him, was a vintner in Valenciennes, Guilliam Vigne, but then the Spanish came, and since they meant either to kill us or convert us, he and Maman fled with the other Walloons to Leiden, and then, when the WIC gave them permission to create a community of their own here in the New World, they were ready to take the gamble."

"What was it like back then?" Anneke asked.

"Ouf! You can't imagine. There was nothing here, *nothing*. That first year we lived in holes in the ground, and then Maman had another baby—you know my brother Jan was the very first boy ever born here—but everything's so much nicer now. You'll see."

Anneke smiled at her uncertainly. "I hope so."

At last, after the girls had been put to bed and Claes and Jacob had gone out to explore, the adults sat down in the front room of the small house to visit. Roelof was awkwardly trying to smoke one of Dirck's long clay pipes—a luxury he hadn't been able to afford in Patria—but Anneke had declined. She would learn to smoke, of course she would, but today she didn't want to embarrass herself.

"So, Roelof," Dirck began, pulling his ladder-back chair closer to the hearth, "what takes you to Rensselaerswyck? There are a few fur traders up by Fort Orange, but otherwise not much going on up there."

"We're not going for peltries. Heer Van Rensselaer means to make his profit from agriculture. He's hired me to manage one of the farms there, the one called De Laetsburg that's across the river from the fort."

"What would possess Van Rensselaer to entrust one of his precious farms to a Norwegian sailor with absolutely no farming experience?"

"Her moeder," Roelof said, nodding toward Anneke.

"Of course." Dirck laughed. "Tryn knows everyone."

"How wonderful that she and your sister will be coming, too," Christine said to Anneke. "We've needed a midwife for so long. I just hope she makes it in time." She patted her own midriff and glanced knowingly at Anneke. Anneke blushed; she hadn't realized she was already showing.

"You know there aren't any other women up there," Dirck said to Anneke. "You'll be the only one."

"No, I didn't know," Anneke answered, "but I was the only woman on the *Eendracht*, and I managed."

"But what terms did Van Rensselaer give you?" Dirck turned back to Roelof. "What would it take to get you to drag your wife and daughters into this wilderness?"

"I think they're pretty good ones," Roelof said, gingerly trying to relight his pipe with a coal from the hearth. "For the next four years I'll be his tenant farmer with a salary of one hundred and eighty guilders per year. Van Rensselaer will provide seed and stock. At the end of my contract, everything I build will belong to him, and I'll return all of his initial investment, but then half of any surplus will be mine."

"You know you're never going to see a stiver of that money, don't you?"

"Oh?" Roelof raised an eyebrow.

"Well, think about it. Everything you take from his warehouse for your personal use, and I mean *everything*, will be deducted from your salary. And then all of the accounts, and I mean *all* of them, will need to be sent back to Patria to be verified. How long did it take you to get here?"

"Not long. Just a couple of months."

"Sixty-five interminable days at sea," Anneke clarified.

"Hmm, that *is* pretty fast. Let's say the average trip takes closer to three months. That means any request from here takes three months to arrive, at least another three months to be chewed over, and yet another three months for any possible decision to get back to us, by which time everything here already will have changed so whatever reply we receive will be irrelevant. And that's why, whether we work for the Dutch West India Company or not, we all live in the Company's town. The director, no matter who he is, has unlimited power."

"Let's hope Rensselaerswyck will be different," Roelof said.

"Maybe it will be, maybe it will, but don't expect to see any silver anytime soon."

"But how can that be?" Anneke cried. "We're counting on that salary. We have nothing of our own. We have children to feed. How will we live?"

"It will be all right." Christine patted her arm. "You will learn to trade for what you need. Look," she said, reaching into a chest and pulling out several strings of beads. "This is sewant. It's made from seashells. The Wilden use it for ceremonial purposes, and we've taken to using it, too, as a form of currency. You'll see tomorrow when we go to buy bread."

"How do you get along with the Wilden?" Roelof asked. "We were told at home that they are gentle and loving."

"Phew," Dirck exhaled. "I suppose some of them might be gentle and loving, but they're people just like anyone else, and some of them can be downright brutal. Europeans have different nations and tongues and religious beliefs, and so do the Wilden. The ones closest to us are called Wecquaesgeek, but each tribe has its own name. After you live here for a while, you'll learn to tell them apart. Up north, where you're going, you'll see mainly Mohicans, but you'll also run into Mohawks who bring their beaver to trade at Fort Orange. A couple of years ago, the Mohawks and the Mohicans were at war with each other, but things are pretty quiet now."

"You may see some River Indians when you sail past Esopus Creek next week," Christine added. "They farm there in the summer."

"What about language?" Anneke asked. "How do they communicate?"

"Here in the south, they all seem to speak some version of the same language. There are all sorts of differences, but they seem to understand each other pretty well . . . just as we Northern Europeans do. Further north, the Mohawks speak a different tongue. Some of our fur traders claim to understand it, but I'm guessing they know only the words they need for trade—beaver, bear, how many, how much."

"But our relations with them are correct," Roelof said. "We haven't taken their land by force, have we?"

"No, it's the WIC's policy to buy their land. Peter Minuit—he's our director—bought the land we're sitting on now for about sixty guilders worth of trade goods. It's hard to say whether it was a fair price or not, but everyone seemed satisfied. The trouble is no one seems to understand what we purchased. The Wilden act like we are their tenant farmers. They come and go as they please, enter our homes, eat our food, even sleep on our floors."

"When you outfit yourselves next week, be sure to take plenty of trade goods—tin mirrors, jaw harps, combs, beads," Christine advised.

"But we're not traders," Roelof protested.

"You won't earn your living by trading, but every interaction with the Wilden will include an exchange of gifts. They will give gifts to you, and you'd better have something on hand to give to them, that's all."

"And don't worry about the Wilden," Christine added. "There are plenty of other things out there that can kill you just as easily."

Anneke looked at her with concern. This was not the reassurance she had been seeking.

Two

DE LAETSBURG FARM

(1630–1632)

The North River

The trip up the North River from Fort Amsterdam to Fort Orange took less than a week. The time they spent on the river sloop felt like a respite to Anneke. Sometimes when the tide was coming in, their small craft sped forward, but as the tide went out again, they began to tack, giving Anneke leisure to observe. Tall rock formations resembling palisades jutted up into the air on their left, and rugged mountains appeared in the distance ahead.

"Oh, Roelof!" she exclaimed, "I never thought it would be so beautiful. Do you imagine this is what the Rhine Valley looks like?" From time to time, she spied deer moving through the trees, and once she caught sight of a bear fishing from the shore. Occasionally she saw smoke rising in the distance and wondered whether it might be coming from Indian encampments. And when they sailed past the mouth of Esopus Creek, she did see people farming there. "Look," she called out to Roelof, "there are women working in the field."

"That must be because the men are all so lazy," he joked. "Maybe we can learn something from them after all."

A few days later, Anneke, sitting in the stern of their sloop, caught sight of the palisaded walls of Fort Orange. Within hours, their captain took advantage of the outgoing tide to bring their vessel to a juddering halt on the muddy bank of the river, and men rushed from the fort to lay planks across the mud for the disembarking passengers.

True to his word, Wolfert Gerritsen was there to meet them, but he seemed tired and out of sorts. The WIC had refused to ship the weapons, farm implements, livestock, and seed that he had been expecting, and Commissary Houten, who was in charge of the sixteen WIC soldiers garrisoned at Fort Orange, was downright hostile to the idea of any Rensselaerswyck colonists settling nearby and reluctant to provide assistance.

"So, what does that mean for us?" Roelof asked.

"Your farmhouse is nearly complete, so at least you'll have a place to stay. I don't have any wheat seed to give you, and for the time being, you're going to have to make do with four horses. I'm trying to purchase additional livestock from settlers on Manhattan, and I'll get them to you as soon as I can, but right now, that's the best I can do."

In the end, it was Commissary Houten, perhaps softened by the sight of Anneke and her girls, who gave Roelof the most useful information about what to expect on the other side of the river. "You'll find the Wilden have already cleared the land," he explained. "They do it by burning the trees, but they leave the stumps in the ground, so you and your lads will want to dig them out, and then in time you'll want to be putting more land under plow, but one step at a time, heh?"

On the day they left the fort for their intended farm, the Commissary sent one of his men to guide them to the farmstead. "Here, mevrouw," he slipped a parcel to Anneke. "This is dried venison. There's plenty of game to be had in those woods, but this will tide you over until you're settled in. Sloops will be arriving frequently for the rest of the summer, and your man can come over to the fort to pick up provisions, but when the river freezes, you'll pretty much be on your own."

Their farm would be on the east side of the North River. It was the whole reason they had come to this land. Carrying Katryn on her hip and pulling Sara by the hand, Anneke followed the others up the embankment with a sinking heart. Her back hurt, and she was fighting bouts of nausea, but at last, just when she thought she could walk no longer, they came to a clearing where blue and yellow wildflowers danced in the wind and filled the air with their scent. On the far side of the clearing she saw a small, swaybacked house-barn. Roelof stopped and pointed to the house. "This is it," he said. "This is where we will make our home." And Anneke smiled, happy for the first time since they left Amsterdam.

The summer was well advanced by the time Wolfert Gerritsen managed to get additional livestock—sheep, cows, and hogs—to Roelof, and there was still the question of what to plant and where to plant it. "Well, we do have some barley," Roelof said to Claes and Jacob. "We might as well give it a try, but I don't know how we're going to get a plow into this ground."

"Why don't we burn off the grass the way the Wilden do?" Claes suggested.

The next day Roelof measured an area that he reckoned could be plowed in about five mornings, checked to see which way the wind was blowing, and strategically set fires in the dry grass. Anneke was the first to notice the wind shifting, and she screamed as the flames came rushing toward the house.

"Sara, run!" she cried, as she scooped up Katryn and fled to a place of safety behind a boulder on the outskirt of the clearing. Roelof and the boys frantically drove the panicking horses and cows in the same direction. Anneke stared in dismay as the fire licked the edges of her doorway. She ran back once to grab the small trunk where most of their clothing was stored, but after that it was too late, and she sobbed as she watched the flames devour their home and everything within.

Roelof held her as she cried. "Come now," he chided. "It's just a building. The next one will be bigger and better. We're all safe, and that's the only thing that matters."

"You don't understand," Anneke cried. "This is the only house I've ever lived in that I've been able truly to call my own."

Wolfert Gerritsen, when he learned of the mishap, quickly rounded up a crew of two farmhands and a carpenter and brought them across the river to see what they could do about repairing the damage.

"Don't worry, it happens to everyone," he said to the chagrined Roelof, "but we'll make the next one out of stone and see if we can't get it to last a little longer."

The hearth and chimney from the old house were still intact, so the men quickly built a living area with the hearth in the middle, a loft overhead for storing grain, and six box beds along the outer walls. Then, during the rest of the warm months, they added a barn with a large threshing floor, stalls for horses and cows, and pens for hogs and sheep. "There now, better than ever," Roelof said. Anneke nodded, but in her heart she still missed their old house.

Anneke had naively thought that when her time came, she would take the sloop to New Amsterdam or at least be able to cross the river to Fort Orange, but one morning when she was out milking, her water burst. “Sara!” she screamed for her oldest daughter, “finish the milking. Don’t let it spoil!” And then she walked, slowly and deliberately, sometimes stopping for a strong contraction, back from the stable into the house. “Katryn,” she said calmly to her three-year-old, not wanting to frighten her, “run fetch Pappa. I need help.” Then she pulled a stool over, sank down on it, supporting her back against the wall, spread her legs wide and began pushing—gently at first and then with greater urgency.

Roelof came running, and for the next two hours he supported her, letting her grip his arm and helping her lean back against the wall and rock forward again to push. At last, he received his new baby daughter, wiped her clean and swaddled her, and gave her to Anneke to suckle. “I know you wanted a boy,” she whispered.

He wiped the sweat from her face and kissed her. “I want any child that God chooses to give us. I’m just sorry you won’t be able sit in bed with pink ribbons on your bonnet as you recover.”

Anneke laughed at the very thought of sitting idle in bed. “And I’m sorry we don’t have a paternity cap for you to flaunt. But it doesn’t matter,” she murmured, drowsily clutching her baby girl to her breast, “we’ll have other chances.” They named the infant Sofia and wanted to call her Fytje, but Katryn couldn’t make the *f* sound, so she became Sytje, and Sytje she would remain.

By their second spring on the farm, Sara and Katryn were old enough to help with chores, but Anneke often found that she could get more done if she sent them “to look for berries.” With the entire farm theirs to explore, every day became a day of discovery.

“Mamma, Mamma!” they cried. “We saw a tiny bear!”

"Bears aren't tiny."

"But we saw one! And it had stripes on its tail and a mask on its face, and three tiny, tiny baby bears walking in a line behind it, and oh! Mamma! if we catch one, can we keep it?"

"Maybe when Baby Sytje is a little bigger. Let's talk about it then, heh?"

And then, "Mamma, Mamma! We saw two royal birds, and one of them was blue and the other red, and they both had crowns on their heads, and we think the blue one is the pappa bird and the red one is the mamma."

"And why do you think that?"

"Because the red one is the prettiest, and we think the mamma should always be the prettiest."

Anneke was pleased by their adventurousness, but she was also mindful of what Christine had warned her about—a poisonous snake that made a noise like a dried gourd, mushrooms that looked good to eat but made you sick—but so far the girls had found only things that were beautiful and enchanting.

But then there came the day when they ran in shouting, "Mamma, Mamma! Wilden!" Anneke, who had been slicing cabbage for *koolsla,* stiffened. Roelof and the others were out spreading manure, too far away to help. Still holding her heavy knife, she walked slowly to the open door and saw at the edge of the clearing a boy of about eight holding two smaller girls by their hands.

"Well, girls. I guess if you have guests, you had best give them something to eat." She cut off large slabs of *roggebrood,* smeared them thickly with butter, and handed them to Sara, who was bouncing up and down in excitement. Then, standing with Katryn in the doorway, ready to intervene at any second, she watched as her six-year-old daughter marched over to the strangers and offered them the dense rye bread with one hand while making an eating gesture with the other.

The small girls tried to run, but the older boy held them fast and stretched out his hand to accept a piece of bread. Then, as Anneke looked on, Sara drew herself up to her full height and said in her best grown-up voice, "Ik heet Sara."

The children looked at Sara in puzzlement, so she tried again. This time she simply put her hand on her chest and said, "Sara." Then she pointed to the boy, who copied her gesture and said, "Kitpul." Seeming pleased with their accomplishment, they both broke out laughing.

Sara apparently wanted more. She gestured toward the entire group and said, "Wilden."

Again, Kitpul copied her gesture, but he said, "Mohican." Then he made a circling gesture that took in the entire farmstead and said, "Swanneken."

Sara hesitated, and Anneke wondered how she would respond. Everyone at the farm spoke Norwegian, but Sara also knew the land they were living on belonged to the Dutch. At last, she said with great dignity, "Europeans."

Roelof was alarmed to learn of the strange visit, but Anneke was quick to reassure him. "They were just children. They were curious. And anyway, if we are to make our home here, we must have good neighbors."

"Children have parents, you know, and there's no reason to suppose they have any love of us."

"And there's no reason to suppose they don't. If the youngsters come again, I don't see any harm in letting our girls spend time with them. I promise I will keep a close eye on everyone."

The following week when Anneke was out in the farmyard straining the morning milk, she was not alarmed to hear the girls cry, "Mamma, Mamma! Wilden!" She again prepared rye bread and butter, but when she looked toward the clearing, she realized that Kitpul was accompanied not by small children but by a young woman. She let Sara carry the bread again, but this time she went with her. When they reached the clearing, Sara, acting as though she were in charge of introductions, put her hand on her mother's hip and said, "Anneke."

"Welanie," Kitpul responded, pursing his lips and jerking his chin toward his companion.

Anneke and Sara shared their bread, and then Welanie opened her *notas*, an elaborately beaded pouch, and poured seeds of maize and squash into her hand. She nodded toward Anneke's kitchen garden and made a digging gesture. She wanted to help with the planting. The two women and the girls worked together for the rest of the afternoon planting mounds of maize alternating with squash while Kitpul "supervised." When their work was finished, Sara whispered, "Mamma! Give her a gift."

Taken unawares, Anneke, without thinking, reached up under her cap, pulled out her bodkin, the long needle she used to lace up her bodice, and handed it to Welanie. The younger woman stared at the strange object for a moment, but then she beamed her thanks. "Wanishi!" They had both touched other worlds.

Kitpul was a frequent guest for the rest of the summer. Sometimes he came alone, sometimes with Welanie, and sometimes with other children. Katryn was still shy around the youngsters, but Sara spent almost all of her time roaming about with her new friends, learning their language and playing their games. Kitpul and the others taught her which plants of the forest were best to eat, which ones could heal, where to catch fish, and how to steal ducks' eggs. They raced toads, and caught fireflies, and sucked honeysuckle together, and Kitpul taught Sara the Mohican names of the strange creatures that had so enchanted her when she first encountered them the previous year. The royal blue bird with its perky crown would always be *tiyas* to her, so much more attractive than *blauwe gaai*. She was disappointed to learn that the royal red bird with its equally perky crown was not the consort of the blue one, but instead the male of a different species. When Kitpul showed her the dull brown female, she cried, "But why? I thought the girls were always supposed to be prettier."

"Not so," Kitpul replied. "The male must always be the boldest."

Welanie, when she visited, worked with Anneke either in the garden or in the cooking area. She prowled around the house, examining unfamiliar objects, lifting the sleeping curtains to peer inside the box beds, and sniffing and tasting anything that Anneke happened to be making. She seemed fascinated by chubby blond Sytje and spent hours helping the infant stand and crawl and tickling her toes. Welanie never came without a gift, usually food, but once a beaded *notas* that became Anneke's dearest treasure, and Anneke, out of gratitude, almost always sent her home with some sort of trinket—once a mirror, another time a comb, and then a paper of pins. She wasn't trading. No, she knew trading was forbidden, but surely there was nothing wrong in making a gift, especially when it came from the heart and she expected no personal gain.

One day toward noon, when Roelof and the boys came home for dinner, Anneke invited Welanie and Kitpul to share their meal. Today, as they so often did, they were having *pannenkoeken*. Welanie watched with interest as Anneke made a thin batter of buckwheat flour, milk, and salt that she cooked in butter in a long-handled pan held over the flame in the hearth. After about an hour, she set a pewter plate with several dozen of the chewy rounds on the barrelhead that served them as a table. Kitpul started to reach for one, but Anneke motioned for him to wait for Roelof to stop whispering into his hat. When the whispering finished, everyone reached for the pancakes at the same time, and then, when they finished eating, Roelof mumbled a few more words, and the men all went back to work. Anneke sent Welanie home that day with a small bag of flour and a knob of butter.

A few days later, Kitpul told Sara that his sister's *pan'kuka* made with spring water were the best he had ever eaten in his whole life. He said they both found it odd that all the farm folk sat down to eat at the same time. As far as Sara could understand, Kitpul's people just kept a pot of something tasty bubbling, and folks ate whenever they were hungry.

Kitpul also questioned Sara about her father's strange behavior at the beginning and the end of the meal. Sara, in halting Mohican, explained that it was customary to ask God's blessing before eating and to give thanks to Him afterward.

Kitpul nodded his comprehension. His people also invoked the spirits on numerous occasions, but he had never seen it done so matter-of-factly.

Several days after the great pancake feast, Welanie and Kitpul arrived bearing a bag of a gritty gray substance that turned out to be maize meal. Welanie, communicating with gestures and with the help of Sara and Kitpul, explained that she wanted to make *sapan*. First, she brought some water to a boil, and then she slowly started adding the maize, stirring until it became a thick porridge. Anneke understood that she had been given a versatile gift. To show her appreciation, she took the iron kettle from her own hearth and offered it to Welanie. She could always get another one from the Company store later.

That evening, Anneke served the porridge from a large bowl. It seemed a little bland to her, so she added salt, and then she made indentations for each of the six people who would be sharing the dish and filled them with buttermilk. Baby Sytje would sit on her lap and eat from her spoon.

"What is this?" Roelof asked with deep suspicion.

"It's called sappaen," Anneke responded. "It's made from maize meal."

"It's actually good," Roelof said after the first bite, clearly surprised.

"It's delicious!" Claes was more enthusiastic. "I bet it would be really good with cheese."

"Would it be possible to make bread from it?" Jacob wondered aloud.

"Oh, no," Anneke explained. "Maize meal is far too coarse. Bread made from it would never rise properly."

When the leaves on the trees turned brilliant red, Welanie showed Anneke how to dry the young maize to preserve it for the cold months. On another day, she and Kitpul built a wooden rack and demonstrated how to cut pumpkin rings so that they, too, could hang and dry. Kitpul, who usually tried to distance himself from women's work, enjoyed the cutting part, so Anneke let him keep her heavy knife.

Then, one day after the leaves had started falling and the first hint of frost was in the air, Kitpul announced with an odd air of excitement that his family would be leaving the following day.

"Leaving?" Sara asked. "I thought you lived here."

"Oh, no," he explained. "Our home by the river is for summer only, just for hunting and fishing. Now we are going to our real home," and he described the longhouses and wigwams of the Mohican, situated on a hilltop and fortified by a triple palisade.

Anneke laughed when Sara told her what Kitpul had said about the winter home of the Mohican. "That can't be right, dear. That sounds like a castle. You must have gotten something wrong."

Three

A WIDER CIRCLE

(1632–1634)

Roelof, arriving home from one of his infrequent trips to Fort Orange, brought with him dried peas and salt pork and welcome news from New Amsterdam. Tryn Jonas and Marritje had safely made the crossing and were now living in a house provided by the WIC not far from the fort.

Anneke had never truly believed she would ever see her family again, and now here they were—a mere river's journey away. "Oh, Roelof!" she exclaimed. "Is there any way we could go to New Amsterdam? I would give anything to see Mamma and Marritje again, and Sytje could be baptized."

"I had the same thought," Roelof said, smiling. "The harvest is in, and the boys can take care of the animals while we're away. There's a sloop that will be returning in two days' time. I've already paid the captain to hold spaces for us and the girls." He started to add, "If that's agreeable to you," but Anneke had already waltzed away, picking up each of her daughters in turn and kissing and hugging them until they squealed.

The return trip to New Amsterdam, like the earlier trip to Rensselaerswyck, took several days, but this time Anneke felt like a different person. The earlier Anneke had been filled with apprehension about their final destination. This Anneke was filled with smiles and songs and eager anticipation. She made a game with the girls of blowing into the sails to see if they could make the sloop go faster, and then she used the passing scenery to entertain them. "Look! What a large flock of pigeons! How many do you think there are? Who can count the most hickory trees? Who can spy a beaver's dam?"

New Amsterdam seemed to them crowded and busy. As they walked up from the river landing, past the gristmill and the fort, onto the market field, they could see new houses being built where once there had been pasture. At last, they reached the small house the WIC had allocated to Tryn Jonas. Tryn shrieked when she caught sight of them and ran to embrace Anneke. Then she held her out at arm's length and examined her. "You're really here," she said. "You're still alive. You made it."

"We made it," Anneke agreed with quiet pride. "And here is your newest granddaughter." She handed the squirming Sytje over to her *oma*.

Marritje was, if anything, even more excited than Anneke. The sisters looked alike—short, with straight blond hair and rosy round cheeks—but Marritje, although younger, was the taller of the two, livelier and more outgoing. After their long separation, they had an almost physical need to talk. Roelof said that being in the same room with them was worse than living in a henhouse, and he took himself off to have a drink with Dirck Holgertsen at one of the quayside taverns.

Marritje described their journey, which, according to her, had been even longer and more hazardous than Anneke's own. "We had scarcely left Texel," she said, "when we were pursued by Dunkirk pirates, and *then* after we outran them and I thought everything was going to be easy-peasy, we ran into a tropical storm—a *hurricane* they called it—that I thought was going to break our ship to little bits."

The next two weeks passed in a whirlwind of activity. Dominee Michaelius baptized Sytje in the upper story of the sawmill where his congregation met. Roelof and Anneke made a solemn commitment to raise their child within the beliefs of the Dutch Reformed Church, and they invited Dirck and Christine to stand with them as witnesses. When the somber event was over, Dirck and Christine invited friends and neighbors back to their place to mark the occasion with an anker of brandy and eel pie and fritters.

On the night of the party, Marritje decided that she would go back to the farm with Anneke and spend the winter there. "Just think how much help I'll be! We'll have so much fun." Once again, Roelof and Anneke outfitted themselves at the WIC warehouse, this time with Marritje in tow.

"We need flour, and sugar, and salt," Anneke explained to Marritje. "I want vinegar, and hard cheeses, and two ankers of brandy. We need duffle to make coats for the children, and we'll take combs, and bodkins, and spoons as gifts for the Wilden."

"Aren't you forgetting something?" Marritje prodded.

"Yes, I need to replace that kettle and the knife I gave away last summer."

"No, silly, Christmas is coming. I am not getting on that sloop unless I know you have ginger, and cinnamon, and wine for a proper celebration."

In Rensselaerswyck, Marritje, still new to the colony, commented on things that for Anneke had already receded into the background. "I can't believe you're burning *wood* in the hearth," she exclaimed. "Back home we only ever burned peat."

"Wood?" Anneke answered absently. "Oh, we always burn wood. We think oak gives a superior heat."

"But won't you run out?"

"Oh, no, there are trees here as far as the eye can see. We'll never be without wood."

Marritje sampled Anneke's *sappaen* and declared it the finest dish she had ever eaten in her life, and she raved about venison. "Just think! Back home only rich people ever get to eat venison, and here we can have it every day."

After a brief supper of bread and weak beer, when all of the daily chores had been done and there was still light enough left in the sky to see, the sisters would sit by the hearth with their mending and reminisce about the life they used to know. Sara would sit on the floor beside them, often with a stocking of her own to darn, and beg Aunt Marritje to tell her over and over about their childhood, about family and friends, and especially about Amsterdam, of which she had only the vaguest memory.

"Well, we lived near Sint Antoniespoort . . ."

"What's that?"

"It used to be a gate in the city wall, but when we lived there, the wall had been torn down, and only the gatehouse was left. It was close to the harbor, and a lot of seafaring folks, especially us Northerners, used to live there."

"Tell me again! Where did Mamma and Pappa get married?"

"Ah, that was the Oude Kerk. It's the most beautiful building in the whole world. It's as big as your whole farmyard, and its tower goes all the way up to the sky, and your mamma and pappa were the most elegant couple you can imagine. Your mamma wore a white gown with a blue underskirt, and she let her hair hang loose and had a crown of flowers, and your oma and I cried so hard because we were so happy for her."

"And then I came along!"

Marritje's face darkened. "Do you remember when you used to have a big sister?"

Sara shook her head.

"Well, baby Lyntje came first, but God took her away, and *then* you and your sisters came to make your parents the happiest people in the world." Marritje didn't explain how much it pained them all to leave little Lyntje behind in the paupers' cemetery.

"And the market! Tell me about the market!" Sara had vivid memories of the sounds and smells of the market even though she had still been wearing leading strings when Anneke took her there for the last time.

"Oh, the market was a special place. You could buy anything there. There used to be fresh fish and oysters and fruit from all over the world." Again, Marritje didn't mention that their own family hadn't been able to afford those wonderful things and that for the most part they had lived on cabbage and *roggebrood*.

Sara, at age six, had her doubts about Sinterklaas, but on December 5, she was just as excited as Katryn to set her shoe filled with carrots and hay for the good man's horse by the massive open hearth. Marritje had been teasing the girls for days, telling them that Sooty Piet would probably leave switches for them because they'd been so naughty, but they both were certain that the shoes would miraculously be filled with treats by morning. Marritje told them that when she and Anneke were little, they used to go from house to house singing Sinterklaas songs and collecting treats from the neighbors. Here, because they had no neighbors, she taught them to sing "Sinterklaas, Good Holy Man," and they marched around the farmyard singing it to the horses and the cows and collecting from each of them a bit of the honey cake that Marritje carried concealed in her pocket.

At last the great day arrived. Snow lay deep on the ground outside, but inside, a fire blazed on the open hearth, and the house smelled of evergreen boughs and gingerbread. The girls found in their shoes real dolls with heads carved from wood that Marritje had brought for them from Amsterdam. She had also managed to conceal in her trunk all manner of sweets—candied cinnamon bark, marzipan shaped like sausages, and salty lozenges of licorice—and she had even smuggled in three gloriously round Brazilian oranges—one for each girl's shoe.

They had a special dinner that day of rich venison with a spicy pepper sauce, and in an effort to be festive, Marritje had had the brilliant idea of making pancakes with a mixture of wheat flour and maize meal bound together with egg and mashed pumpkin.

After dinner, the girls stood by the hearth and sang their new song in their sweet, clear voices:

Sinterklaas, good holy man,
Put your best robe on.
Ride away to Amsterdam,
To Amsterdam from Spain . . .

"Do you know, girls," Marritje asked, "the story of Saint Nicholas?" They did, but they wanted to hear it again. "Well," she began, "once upon a time, a very long time ago, there lived three beautiful sisters . . ."

"Just like us!"

"Exactly like you! And they wanted to get married, but because they were poor, they had no dowries."

"What's a dowry?"

"Something that girls used to need a long time ago in order to get married." Marritje was not about to get into the commercial aspects of matrimony. "So one day, Saint Nicholas overheard the three girls talking about how sad they were because they could never have husbands. That very night he took three balls of gold"—she held up the three oranges—"and threw them through the window so they landed right in the girls' shoes." She demonstrated, tossing the oranges deftly across the hearth and missing only twice. "The next morning, the girls were rich, and they all found wonderful husbands and had dozens of babies and lived happily ever after."

The days between Sinterklaas and the end of the year passed quickly. There were still chores to be done, but Roelof and the boys found time to play *kolf* on the frozen pond, and the girls made up sliding games of their own. Anneke and Marritje cleaned the house and cooked and baked without restraint. Christmas Day was solemn and subdued, but Marritje, who had a glorious voice, treated them to "O Christmas Night, More Beautiful Than Any Day," making the octave jump in the first measure as easily as any chorister, and then Anneke told the girls the familiar story of the long-ago trip to Bethlehem and the birth in the manger.

A New Year's Eve storm with sleet and ice kept them from building a bonfire, but toward midnight, the weather cleared, and they went outside to welcome the new year by banging on pots and pans and shooting into the air. They could hear answering shots from Fort Orange across the river.

"Wouldn't it be funny," Claes said, "if the Wilden were attacking, and we didn't pay any attention because we thought everybody was celebrating?"

Anneke shushed him with an angry look. Not funny, not funny at all, not at all a good way to welcome the year of Our Savior 1632.

Toward the end of February, when the ice on the river had started to break, Marritje began making plans to return to New Amsterdam.

"Anneke, do you remember Tymen Jansen?"

"The carpenter? Yes, why?"

"He gave me this handkerchief."

"Sister! You haven't!"

"Had conversation of the flesh?" Marritje mocked. "Maybe . . ."

"Does Mamma know?"

"Not yet, but we plan to publish banns just as soon as I get back."

Anneke stood on tiptoe to kiss her little sister on the cheek. "Then I'm very happy for you. Very happy indeed."

Wolfert Gerritsen summoned Roelof and several others to the fort and explained to them that Heer Van Rensselaer wanted his fledgling fiefdom to institute Dutch forms of governance. He, Wolfert, would remain director, of course, but from now on they would also have a proper burgher council headed by a *schout* who would prosecute evildoing and five *schepenen* who would advise the director on questions that he brought before them and sit in judgment on miscreants apprehended by their *schout*. The men he had summoned that day had been selected to fill those roles.

"Don't you look handsome!" Anneke exclaimed when Roelof returned from the swearing-in. "I wish we had a proper mirror."

Roelof was modeling the elegant black hat with silver ribbon that he had received as a symbol of his new authority.

"Just think! Roelof Jansen van Masterland—Magistrate

of Rensselaerswyck, keeper of the peace, defender of the innocent, dispenser of justice."

Even though Roelof was flattered, he knew he had been chosen simply because there weren't enough men to go around, so he tried to make light of it. "Yeah, next thing you know I'll be wearing a peruke, heh?"

"And why not? I think they're ever so elegant. Tell me again about the swearing-in ceremony."

"Well, Rutger Hendricksen is schout now, and, oh! Anneke, you should have seen him. He had a silver rapier and a black hat with a *plume*. Anyway, he gave the five of us our hats and had us recite the oath."

"And what did you promise to do?"

"We swore that we would pass honest judgment not only between farmer and farmer but also between patroon and farmer."

"That ought to be easy since the patroon has never set foot in this place."

"And the farmers are too spread out to quarrel."

In midsummer, Welanie visited the farm once more carrying a fat baby boy in a cradle board on her back. She admired Baby Sytje's stumbling attempts to walk and laughed at the padded pudding cap that Anneke had made to keep the child from banging her head when she fell, and Anneke nodded her approval at the ingenious cradle board that served to swaddle Welanie's infant while leaving his mother's hands free to work. Anneke gave the boy a child's cap that she somehow doubted would get much use, but it was the only thing she had to hand. They never did learn the baby's name.

Now that Welanie had a family of her own, they didn't see much of her, but Kitpul still stopped by every week or so.

Sara, who was almost eight, had chores of her own, including milking. Kitpul tasted the warm milk once and spat it out, but he never seemed to tire of watching the small blond girl manipulate the massive bovines. Afterward, when she would call, "Pooooeeess-poes-poes-poes," he would laugh to see tiny creatures that looked like miniature pumas come running toward her with their tails straight up in the air begging for a sip of milk. Sara wanted to give him one of the kittens, but Roelof told her it would not fare well among the Indians' dogs.

Anneke permitted Sara to walk with Kitpul as far as the boulder at the edge of the clearing, and the two of them often sat there and simply talked. By now, Sara was skilled enough in Mohican to be able to describe things that she remembered from the Old World and to ask Kitpul about his own past. He told her he had never known a world without Swanneken, but some of the older people remembered seeing a tall ship for the first time and thinking it must be some monster from the sea or, more likely, a ghost come from hell. He listened to Sara describing a forest of tall ships and stone buildings many times bigger than the farmhouse, with towers that stretched almost to the sky, and he thought that surely her limited language skills had caused her to misspeak.

Kitpul, now eleven, told her what little he remembered about the war with the Mohawks, how frightening it had been and how many people had died, including his own father and an older brother. He explained that the Mohican had three clans. As far as Sara could make out, he said that because his mother was a Turtle, he would have to marry a Wolf or a Bear. There used to be more Mohican than there were now, he told her, but the older people said a great illness came at about the same time as the tall ships, and then many more died in the war.

Sara told him how much she used to love the public market in Amsterdam when she was little. She described crowds of people from all over the world, all of them wearing different costumes and speaking different languages.

"How many of them do you think will come here?" he asked.

"I don't know. Does it matter?"

"I was just wondering where they all would live."

Sara gestured to the woods beyond. "How far does this go on?"

"I don't know. Probably forever."

"Then there should be enough room for all of us, don't you think?"

Kitpul started as though he had just heard a sharp noise, but then he shook it off and smiled at her. "I guess so, yes."

Marritje came again the following spring and brought with her one of Tryn's old birthing chairs. The girls were glad to see their vivacious aunt, and Roelof was relieved that Anneke would have her sister with her this time. Anneke noticed a new sadness in Marritje, which she attributed to a recent miscarriage, but Tymen, according to Marritje, was the most wonderful man in the world.

"Just imagine!" she bragged, "he is so talented that he has already been appointed chief shipwright."

The birthing chair was to Anneke's eyes a thing of beauty. Tryn had had it crafted to her specifications in Amsterdam by a joiner who owed her a birthing fee. She asked him to make it light and foldable so she could carry it to her clients, but she also had notches made on the arms and the footrests so they could be adjusted for the mother's height and then, her own innovation, she had handles added for the mother to grip as she labored. Anneke's travail was longer and more difficult this time, but in her mother's chair and with her sister's help she finally brought a strong baby boy into the world.

"And this time," Marritje informed her, "you're really going to stay in bed and rest, and look!"—she dove into her traveling bag and pulled out a mysterious packet—"I've even brought mace and cinnamon and cloves. Give me some eggs, and sugar, and sweet wine, and I'll make you a proper kandeel to give you enough strength to nurse ten baby boys!"

Anneke smiled her thanks and then handed the swaddled infant to Roelof. "Here is your son," she said proudly. "Let's name him Jan, after both of our fathers."

Roelof lay awake, staring into the darkness. He could tell from Anneke's breathing that she, too, was awake, so at last he spoke, "They're not going to renew my contract."

"What!" Anneke sat up so abruptly that she hit her head on the frame of the box bed. "They can't do that! This is our home. We've made this place. You're a schepen, for Heaven's sake. Why would they do such a thing?"

"I don't know. Sometimes I think Van Rensselaer just likes to move people around. I know there were a few complaints about me in the past, but never anything serious."

"What complaints?"

"Well, a couple of years ago, he was unhappy because I hadn't put in enough winter wheat."

"That wasn't your fault. Wolfert Gerritsen didn't get the seed to you in time. And anyway, let the old goat try clearing and planting this land himself, and see how much he gets done."

"And there was another, more recent one I didn't want to tell you about. He said we used up our supply allowance too quickly. He seemed to think either that we'd been trading with the Wilden or that we'd been supporting your mother and sister."

"That's absurd! We're supposed to be able to take supplies for our needs, and we *need* to show our gratitude to the Wilden. We'd be lost without them. And we've never given anything to my family. My sister has been here twice, and both times she's worked just like any day laborer. Are we not supposed to feed her?"

"I know. I just don't know what to do."

"What do you want to do?"

"There's talk of starting a new farm nearer to Fort Orange. I don't know who the tenant would be, but it's been suggested that I could work there and guard the house and cattle at night."

"After being tenant on your own farm? After everything that we've accomplished here? I couldn't bear the thought of living on another Rensselaerswyck farm like a common laborer."

"I wouldn't like it either. The WIC is always hiring on Manhattan. Let me see what I can find there."

That night Anneke cried herself to sleep in Roelof's arms, but the next morning she made herself smile as she explained their grand decision to the children. "Just think! Baby Jan can be baptized, and we can all get to see Oma Tryn and Auntie Marritje every day, and we'll have lots of new friends and neighbors, and we'll even be able to buy pretzels anytime we want. Won't it all be so much fun?"

Four

ANOTHER MISSION

(1637–1641)

New Amsterdam

On the day Roelof died, Anneke was sitting in the scullery behind their new house skinning rabbits. The last three years had been good to her and her sister. Marritje's Tymen had been awarded a good-sized parcel of land near the fort, and then, after many disappointments, God had finally blessed them with a curly-haired baby girl, whom they called Elsie. And Roelof, too, after working for the WIC for two years, had been rewarded for his service with a patent for thirty-four morgens of his own land. It wasn't the best land for farming—partly swamp, partly rock, and inconveniently far from the fort—but they began clearing and planting and then, as time permitted, they built their new home, where Baby Annetje was born.

As Anneke started to skin the last rabbit, she heard shouts from the field and could see men running toward the house carrying something, but it wasn't until they were almost upon her that she saw their burden was Roelof. In the confused yelling, she could make out only one word: snake. She dropped to her knees beside him. His leg was red and swollen, his pulse rapid, and his breathing shallow, and before she even had a chance to wipe his brow, or hold his hand, or tell him how much she loved him, she saw the light fade from his blue-blue eyes, and he was gone. She buried her face in her apron and screamed. Sara, seeing her mother's distress, ran unasked to fetch her *oma*.

"Come quick!" she cried, "Pappa is sick, and Mamma needs your help."

Anneke was still sobbing beside her dead husband when Tryn shook her roughly by the shoulder and said, "Stop it! Man's days are numbered. Roelof is with God now, and it's a sin to grieve."

Anneke looked at her mother in astonishment and for the first time in her life spoke to her in anger. "*You* stop it, Mamma! I know Roelof is in God's Hand, and I must not grieve for him, but surely I can grieve for *myself*. I have five children and a poorly cultivated farm, and now our provider is *gone*. The only man I've ever loved, the only person in the whole world who cared for me more than he did for himself is *gone*. How can we live without him?"

Tryn wiped the tears from her daughter's face and said more gently, "Come now, there's work to be done. You must prepare his body for burial, and he will need a coffin."

"I can't afford a coffin. We'll have to make do with a shroud."

"Daughter, this is Roelof we're talking about. We have to do right by him. Tymen will make a coffin for you, and I have plenty of credit for the other things we need." Then she turned to Marritje, who had also come running, and said, "I want you to go to the WIC warehouse and get flour and sugar for the dood koekjes—I think about a hundred—and we'll need mulled wine. Let's see, I can arrange for the gravedigger to open the ground for him, and I can ask Dominee Bogardus to make a few remarks at the graveside."

"What about the aanspreker, Mamma?" Marritje asked. "Don't we need to send someone through the town to tell people when the burial will be."

"That we do," Tryn said, nodding. "And we need some sort of memento for the more important guests. Silver spoons are too costly, but I think handkerchiefs are always nice. Sara and Katryn can embroider them with Roelof's initials while we prepare the food. Come now, let's get to work."

For the next two days the women, assisted by Sara and Katryn, worked frantically while Sytje took care of five-year-old Jan, two-year-old Cousin Elsie, and three-month-old Baby Annetje. Anneke herself worked mechanically with the same thoughts running through her mind like a shuttle across a loom: mix the dough, sin to grieve, pat the dough, sin to grieve, mark the dough, sin to grieve, bake the dough, sin to grieve. Finally, when she had no more thoughts and no more tears, she abandoned herself to the rhythm of the work and began to experience relief.

On the day of the burial, Claes, Jacob, Tymen, and Dirck Holgertsen carried Roelof's coffin. Five-year-old Jan walked with his Uncle Tymen, resting his small hand on the underside of the coffin as though assisting his father on his final journey. After the men left for the burial ground, the women sat down for a brief moment before the onslaught they knew would follow. Tryn inspected her grandchildren's attire and told Sara to tie a black ribbon around Annetje's swaddling.

The guests began to trickle in, and soon the party was in full swing. Tryn noticed with satisfaction that Director Wouter van Twiller and Dominee Everardus Bogardus had both joined them. The director and the dominee had arrived on the same ship nearly four years ago and had been thick as thieves ever since. The two most powerful men in the colony, they still seemed like boys to Tryn. Wouter was easy to understand. Fat and comfortable, he was more interested in enriching himself than he was in running the colony, but the dominee was more of a mystery. His ordinary name, as everyone knew, was Evert Willemsen Bogart, but as a man who had attended university, he was entitled to the Latin name Everardus Bogardus as well. He was popular, especially among the younger women of the colony who admired his comely features and his refined manners, but Tryn was a little bit afraid of him. He had a lively wit and a sharp tongue, and when he had been drinking, as he had today, he would sometimes home in on things that other people would just as soon not have remembered. He would pick at mental scabs until they bled, and then those very people who would have been flattered to be his friend would mistake his jests for jabs and turn bitterly against him. It was, Tryn thought, probably a hazard of his profession.

After the last cookie had been eaten, the last handkerchief bestowed, and the last guest had left, Tryn sat down with Anneke and Marritje and said, "Here's what we must do. Anneke, you need to marry."

Anneke looked at her dully and said, "I know that, Mamma. I've accepted a gift of cloth from Jacob Goyversen."

"Oh, good!" Marritje approved. "Jacob's such a nice man, and a senior farmhand is almost certainly the best person to take over the farm."

Tryn was less enthusiastic. "Jacob *is* a nice man, but I think you can do better. Look around you, Anneke. There are almost no women in this colony. You're healthy and fertile, and you control a sizable amount of land. Many men will think you a good match."

"I won't marry for money, Mamma. I'm not mercenary."

"You're not mercenary, but you came here to make a better life for your children, and right now the best thing you can do for them is to marry well. And I'll tell you another thing. You have but one son who will not be able to support you for another fifteen years, but you also have four beautiful, intelligent girls who are close to marriageable age. Those girls are your fortune, Anneke. Marry them well, and you will never need to fear for the future again."

"But what about Jacob?"

"I'm sure he has expectations, but promise me you will make no commitment to him for at least three more months, and if during that time, any man of substance, a member of the council, say, or a merchant, makes a proposal to you, promise me you will at least consider it."

A mere five weeks later, Anneke was spreading her linen out to bleach in the spring sun, when she saw the dominee come riding along the dusty road to her house. At first she was startled, thinking she must have fallen behind in her tithing or committed some other infraction, but then she realized he was simply making a courtesy call to see how the family was dealing with its recent loss. She straightened her cap and hurried to greet him, offered him some good beer and cheese, and sat down to endure what she assumed would be a brief amount of small talk.

She thanked him for his assistance with Roelof's burial, and then they chatted a bit about the children. Yes, Sara was already eleven, such a help with Baby Annetje. True, Jan was too young to step in as man of the house. At last, she ran out of topics and fell silent, hoping to force him to speak.

He stammered a bit and then began, "It has come to my notice that you, living out here on your own . . . Actually, I noticed that we both have certain assets . . . I was thinking there might be some benefit, perhaps some profit to both of us in managing them jointly."

Anneke was puzzled. She knew the dominee had some land holdings, but they were out on the Long Island, nowhere near her own. Still . . .

"Well, it's true it's difficult for me to manage this place on my own. What did you have in mind—hiring a joint manager?"

"Uh, I was thinking of a more spiritual conjoining."

Anneke looked up in surprise and burst out laughing. "Evert Willemsen! Are you asking me to *marry* you?"

He blushed and looked at the floor.

"Why would you *do* such a thing? I'm older than you. I have five children. I'm illiterate, can't even speak proper Dutch. I'm *Lutheran*."

As Anneke's tirade intensified, Evert began to smile. He knew he was considered the most eligible bachelor in the colony, and here the only woman he had ever offered his hand to was trying to talk him out of it. At last, he interrupted, "Anna Jans, man needs a helpmate. You are a woman of good character. You will steady me and give me sons, and I promise I will be good to you and to your children. I will make sure that the girls all make good marriages and that Jan has a fitting trade. And I promise they will all learn to read and write."

Anneke stared at him for a moment in stupefaction, but then she reached for the brandy flask and grinned. "All right, Evert Willemsen, let's drink to that."

The following morning, Evert, still in his shirt, sat on Anneke's old trunk looking pale and a trifle fragile. Anneke, neatly dressed and annoyingly cheerful, bustled about making him a breakfast of weak beer and bread.

"I've already sent for the weesmeester," she announced.

Evert was a little slow-witted that morning. "We're not even married yet. What do we need the orphan master for?"

Anneke laughed at what she supposed was a joke. "You know I won't be permitted to marry until the rights of Roelof's children have been secured."

The *weesmeester* assessed Roelof's estate at two thousand guilders—half for Anneke and two hundred apiece for each of his five children. Of course, the land would need to be sold before any money could be distributed, so for the time being Anneke remained as penniless as ever.

And one other legal detail needed to be dealt with. If Anneke had been educated and wealthy, she might have preferred to retain control of her own estate, but Evert was so very superior to her in education and experience that she chose to accept him as her husband and guardian. Henceforth, he would represent her in court, and Roelof's Farm would be known as Dominee's Bouwery.

Wouter teased Evert for marrying an old woman for her land. Evert, as usual, deflected the comment with a joke. "Oh, yes, I'm sure that land is going to be worth a fortune someday."

Marritje teased Anneke for marrying a boy who still wanted mothering. Anneke thought there might be a bit of truth there, but she suspected that the bigger draw for Evert might have been her children. He couldn't bear seeing five orphans at the mercy of the Orphan Court and would do anything in his power to protect them—even if it meant marrying their mother.

Anneke never quite got used to her new role as *predikantsvrouw*. In their small community, everyone knew everybody else's business, but the preacher's wife was subject to particular scrutiny. She now attended numerous church services throughout the week and twice on Sunday, and Evert expected her to sit close to the pulpit in front of the entire congregation. She had new dresses in somber colors made for herself and the girls and a proper suit of clothes for Jan, and when she thought no one was looking, she would practice the pious expressions she thought her fellow churchgoers expected her to wear while listening to her husband's exhortations.

The parsonage itself was situated directly across from the WIC houses. It wasn't particularly grand, but it was larger than any other house that Anneke had ever lived in before, and its long orchard looked out on the market field. It had started out with two rooms on either side of a hearth but now also had steps to an upper story for storage and sleeping, a covered walkway on the west side of the house, and a proper stoop where Anneke could sit of an afternoon and visit with passersby. The front room was dominated by a table covered with Turkish carpet, where Evert had placed his dearest possession, a massive book bound in leather with brass corners and clasps. "This is it," he proudly told Anneke. "Twenty years in the making and published only last year. This is the entire scripture translated into Dutch so that any man, woman, or child can read and understand the Word of God. You have to learn to read."

"Me?" Anneke laughed. "Too old a dog."

"Oh, I could teach you," he said with confidence, "but what we really need is a schoolmeester. I asked Wouter to hire one two years ago, and I'm still waiting."

As preacher's wife, Anneke found that the credit she formerly had to beg for was now readily extended. Hendrick the Baker set aside the softest loaves of white bread for her, and Frans the Butcher made sure she received the plumpest sausages. But, as she quickly learned, she had new obligations as well. Godparents were regarded as a popish superstition, but no parent ever felt comfortable presenting his infant for baptism without the support of witnesses. Prestigious parents wanted prestigious witnesses, and none was in greater demand than the wife of Dominee Bogardus. And Evert himself often asked her to stand witness to the baptism of African children whose parents lived in the WIC slave house.

"How many African children have you baptized?" she once asked him.

"I don't know, quite a few. Maybe I should start keeping a record?"

In time, she became fond of Evert, learned to love him even, and he never failed to surprise her. Once when Anneke ripped her skirt on a nail, he commanded, "Don't move!" He whipped out needle and thread from the table drawer, sat cross-legged on the floor next to her, and within minutes smacked her bottom, saying, "Good as new. Off you go."

No one liked feasting and fun more than Evert, but following every banquet, he inveighed against the evils of gluttony and intemperance. When they dined with Wouter, as they so frequently did, the two men behaved like boys, laughing and jesting, trading insults, and sometimes coming to blows. Anneke was alarmed when Wouter drew his sword and chased Evert down the street for saying he had the morals of a billy goat, but Evert just laughed and said, "Aw, no harm done, just having fun. Good times, heh?"

On a blustery March morning, Anneke joined the crowd gathered on the strand to greet the *Haring* and the *Dolphyn*. The arrival of any ship caused excitement, but these two were of particular interest because Wouter had been recalled, and the new Director of the Colony would soon be making his first appearance.

Evert was to be part of the official welcoming party, so Anneke walked with him as far as the landing and then turned to see who else she knew in the crowd. Soon she spotted her mother standing with Marritje and Tymen.

"Hoi, Anneke," her sister hailed her. "Evert's going to miss Wouter, heh?"

"I suppose so," Anneke answered. "I just hope the new one drinks less."

"Or at least that he can hold it better," Tymen said.

"What are you doing about Roelof's salary?" Tryn wanted to know.

"Evert has given Wouter a Power of Attorney to collect it. He says that if anyone can pry a stiver out of the WIC, it's Wouter."

"Mamma," Marritje interrupted. "Tell us what you know about the new man."

Tryn, who knew all the gossip, said, "Well, I hear he went bankrupt in La Rochelle."

Tymen nodded. "That sounds about right. I don't see how they could get anyone competent to come here."

Anneke suspected the new director had gotten his position the same way Wouter had—through a relative on the board, but she said only, "I just hope he knows how to get along with the Wilden."

At last, the man they had all been waiting for, Willem Kieft, disembarked. His autocratic bearing made a bad impression on Anneke. "Look at that pointed beard and waxed mustache!" she exclaimed to Marritje. "Vain and arrogant, I should think. He looks like a fox come to guard the chickens."

After Wouter had exchanged formalities with his replacement, and Evert had entreated God to bless the colony with wise and benevolent governance, the crowd got back to waiting.

Tryn was excited to welcome the colony's first *heelmeester*.

"He's German," she explained to her daughters. "Meester Hans Kierstede. It's about time we had a proper barber-surgeon in this town."

And Evert was pleased to see Adam Rolantsen, the man they had sent back to Patria two years ago to be licensed as *schoolmeester*, arrive on the same ship. "Meester Adam!" he greeted him. "Welcome back! You must come to the parsonage and stay with us until you get settled. We'll want to start the schooling next week, heh?"

Meester Adam's stay at the parsonage lasted nearly four months. He spent most of that time squabbling with the councilmen about the terms of his employment. They put a cap on how much he could charge per pupil, but, as he was fond of pointing out, no one said anything about accepting gifts.

Anneke found the man annoying in the extreme and couldn't wait to get rid of him. At meals, he addressed all of his remarks to Evert and seldom looked in her direction, but he felt fine about asking her to do his laundry, mend his clothing, and adjust her cooking to his liking. "Perhaps a little more salt next time," he would say to no one in particular, grimacing over a bowl of pea porridge that she had set in front of him.

He treated Evert with great deference, however, agreeing with every idea that he raised. All children would be taught to read. Some, whose parents were willing to pay extra, would also learn to write, and for an additional fee, merchants' sons might study ciphering. Each school day would start with reading from the Bible and end with the singing of some verses from a psalm.

The only time Anneke ever heard any serious disagreement between them was when Adam learned that African children would also be attending his classes.

"Surely you jest, Dominee. It would distract the other children to have pupils so little suited for learning in their midst."

"I am every bit in earnest," Evert said firmly. "Those children have all been baptized, and they must learn the catechism as well as my own stepchildren."

When classes finally got underway, they were held in the rickety wooden church on the strand. Parents paid however they could—with beaver, sewant, firewood, produce—and those who had no means to pay at all were assisted by the deacons. Anneke's own school-age children paid their way by going over early to lay a fire and set out slates and primers to make ready for each day's lesson.

Anneke, who had never attended school, expected great things, and every afternoon when her children came home for dinner, she would quiz them on what they had learned, but they all, even Sara, who was the oldest, answered, "Nothing. Nothing special," or even more annoyingly, "I forget."

After two months of hearing that nothing memorable ever happened at school, Anneke decided to see for herself. She waited until midmorning when lessons would be well underway and then walked around the corner toward the church, but as she got closer to the wooden building, she heard an unearthly hubbub of shrieks, laughter, crying, and jeers. Opening the door, she saw about thirty children for the most part doing whatever they wanted, but her attention was arrested by the sight of her own Sara, her blue kerchief standing out against the yellow of her blouse like a bright flame, standing in front of the teacher's lectern with her fists clenched, and her six-year-old Jan howling in pain as the *meester* smacked his open palm with a wooden spoon.

It was unthinkable that she should do anything to undermine the authority of the teacher, so instead she put her arm around Sara's shoulder and then reached out her hand for Jan. "I'm sorry to interrupt, mynheer," she said meekly, "but my husband has asked me to fetch the children for dinner." And then, as Meester Adam continued to glare at her, she added sweetly, "And the dominee wishes to invite you to dine with us this Sunday after service."

Back home, she sat her children down and listened to their tales of woe, and then she said, "Look, this is what we must do. Tomorrow, Sara, you must tell Meester Adam that your vader is concerned about his heavy teaching load and he has instructed you to take the younger pupils, the ones Jan's age, and work with them in a separate group. If you make a game of learning, you can keep them all quiet and happy. And you, Katryn, must do the same thing with the children who are Sytje's age. Then Meester Adam can work on ciphering with the older boys. Who knows? He might even be good at it."

"And then will the beatings stop?"

"No, a schoolmeester must never spare the rod, but if there is less disorder, there will be fewer reasons to punish, and at least you can keep your own little brother out of trouble."

Anneke was impressed by her husband's erudition, but sometimes she thought he didn't have the good sense of a goose. He was a kind and generous man who would lend money to absolutely anyone. And he took his responsibilities seriously, especially the requirement that he admonish with God's Word anyone who desired such admonition or who, in Evert's opinion, needed it. Now Anneke, although an unlettered woman, knew that it was never a good idea to admonish someone who owed you money, but Evert saw no connection between the blistering sermon he delivered on the grievous misconduct of the infidel Turk, Anthony van Salee, and his equally awful wife, Griet Reyniers, and the Turk's refusal to pay off his debt of three hundred guilders.

Anneke wasn't able to attend council meetings herself, but there were plenty of people who were happy to tell her what went on there. As far as she could tell, the whole thing had started last week when Griet had complained that Evert had an outstanding bar tab of seven guilders. A reasonable person, of course, would have just handed over some sewant and been done with it, but Evert, feeling his honor impugned, swore an oath that he had no such debt, and things escalated. Evert delivered an incendiary sermon, truly one of his more salacious ones, and then submitted a request to the council for the recovery of his three hundred guilders. The Turk, who respected the laws neither of man nor of God, responded to the summons, saying he would rather lose his head than pay the dominee in this wise and adding that Evert must first declare before the director and his council that Anthony and his wife were honorable people, and then he would see what might be done about the money.

It was too late for Evert to back down, so instead he found witnesses to Griet's misdeeds who were willing to swear before the council that Evert had slandered no one and the Turk, by the way, still owed him three hundred guilders. A midwife declared that Griet had asked whether her newborn resembled her husband—a provocative question since Anthony was a Moor. And Meester Adam affirmed that when the *Zoutberg* was leaving harbor in 1633, the sailors had yelled, "Whore, whore, two pound's butter whore" at Griet, who lifted her skirts and slapped her bottom at them, and then *today*, Griet raised the stakes by leveling the same charge against Anneke. Witnesses were quickly found to testify that Anneke had merely been lifting the hem of her skirt to get it out of the mud.

"So did you do it?" Evert winked.

"Maybe." Anneke winked back. "Just a little."

On one of those long summer evenings that seem to go on forever, Anneke and Evert sat by their now cool hearth sharing a pint and a pipe. Soon it would be time either to go to bed or to waste a candle. Evert sat silently in the dusk, staring at the floor.

"You seem melancholy," Anneke prompted.

He shrugged. "Sometimes I feel like such a fake."

"You seem pretty real to me," she said, grinning.

"You know I was an orphan." Anneke nodded. "My father was a cobbler, and I always assumed that he died of drink. I had a stepfather, but the plague took both him and my mother, and my brothers and I all went to the orphanage. People were good to us there—you remind me a little of the matron—but we had porridge and bread for every blessed meal, and every day I was there I spent wishing I could be somewhere, *anywhere* else. When I was fifteen, I was apprenticed to a tailor . . ."

Anneke looked at him with new understanding.

"My master was a good man—Gysbert Albertsen his name was, used to read the Bible to me—but I sat cross-legged by the window all day, every day, breaking my back and ruining my eyes, and I kept thinking: *God does not want me to be doing this.*"

As Evert's mood grew darker in the fading daylight, Anneke silently lit a candle. She did not want to interrupt.

"I kept imagining all sorts of things that God might do to change my lot in life—none of them remotely possible—until I had the thought that He might strike me deaf and dumb, dead as it were, and then I might be able to come back to life a new person respected by others and able to lead them in the Way of God. I thought about it over and over until it almost seemed real, and then it happened."

"What happened?"

"I fell very ill. For nine days I couldn't eat or drink. For several months at a time I became deaf and mute, blind at times. Once again, I stopped eating and drinking until I saw an angel, who told me clearly that God wanted me to preach His Word. During each of these episodes, I wrote copiously—things that seemed important at the time but seem childish to me now, you know: 'O woe to men of pride and wantonness.' Rector Zas collected my drivel and published it as a pamphlet. He permitted me to attend Latin School and then persuaded the city fathers to award me a scholarship to study theology at the University of Leiden."

"That's marvelous." Anneke was filled with admiration.

Evert shook his head. "I hated it there. No matter how smart I was or how hard I studied, I was always the scholarship boy, and then one of the bullies discovered the pamphlet. He showed it to the other kids and told them I was a fraud. I wanted to get as far away from Leiden as possible, so when I heard that the Dutch West India Company was trying to recruit a ziekentrooster for Mouri, I applied."

Anneke knew that a comforter of the sick could do almost everything that a dominee could except baptize and give communion. "So you never finished university?" she asked.

"No, but the entire time I was in Africa, I studied night and day. And then when I heard there was a possibility of being posted to an even *more* remote location, I rushed back to Amsterdam and was examined and ordained as quickly as possible. I have fought so hard to be Everardus Bogardus, the dominee of Manhattan, but every time I set foot outside of this door, I imagine people looking at me and seeing Evert the cobbler's boy. And to this good day I will never know whether

God speaks *through* me or whether I say and do the things I *imagine* He would want me to say."

What an extraordinary man I've married, Anneke thought. She put her arm around his shoulder and kissed his head. "He would say you are a good man doing the best you can to make the world a better place."

A few moments later, she reached over and touched his knee. "May I ask you a question?"

He nodded.

"About Griet Reyniers?"

"Griet!" he exploded. "That whore!"

"Why do you call her whore? What knowledge do you have of her?"

"Wouter had her."

"Or so he says. Do you have any personal experience?"

"Of course not!"

"Evert," she asked very softly so that he was forced to listen. "Is it possible you had a few drinks at Griet's place and forgot to pay her?"

"Never!" he blustered, but then he understood what she was saying and blushed and looked down at the floor.

The next morning early, before there were any customers about, Anneke went to Griet's Tavern. She caught her sweeping the stoop, her son, brown like his father, playing on the ground next to her. Seeing Anneke, Griet gestured angrily with her broom, but Anneke made a calming gesture and approached anyway.

"Griet," she began, "I want you to know that my husband is not a perjurer. He does not acknowledge any debt to you, but I believe there may be some misunderstanding on *your* part, and I want to use my own money to make it right." She held out four strings of sewant. "Will this be enough?"

Speechless for once, Griet nodded, and so for the time being equilibrium was restored to the colony.

Anneke had seen men and women hanged before, but she had too much imagination to find the gyrations of the slowly strangling victims comic. Still, hangings were meant to be edifying, and since Evert was required to attend, she felt obliged to go also. Eight-year-old Jan had begged to go with her, but the January air was so biting and cold that she decided to leave all of the children at home.

The man who was to be hanged, Manuel de Gerrit de Reus, was well-known and well-liked. Manuel was one of the senior WIC slaves, taken, according to his telling, from a captured Portuguese galleon and brought with several other captives to labor for the Company, clearing its land and building its fort. A man of great size and strength, he was a valued laborer, and Anneke knew that the decision to part with him must have been painful for Director Kieft.

The crime for which Manuel was to die was an odd one, and the manner of his conviction odder still. When Jan Premero, another slave, had been discovered murdered in the slave house, a group of nine other slaves with Manuel at their head had come forward and confessed as a group. The council was dumbfounded. By law, they were required to hang murderers, but the idea of losing nine of their most valuable possessions was deeply upsetting. "Slaves are duplicitous," Director Kieft fulminated. "They know we can't kill all nine of them, and they're only doing this to protect the guilty one. Slaves' testimony is valid only when obtained under torture. I say we torture the lot of them."

"Wait!" Evert intervened. "Let God reveal the culprit. Let the men draw straws." Nine straws were drawn, and Manuel, possibly with some sleight of hand, ended up with the shortest one.

The atmosphere on the strand, despite the bitter January cold, was almost festive. A pancake maker had set up a brazier and was raking in stivers and sewant selling her greasy treats to the chilly spectators. Many parents had brought their little ones thinking they might learn a valuable lesson from the dance of death that lay ahead. A huge gibbet, where the tarred bodies of pirates could be displayed, had been erected at the tip of the strand facing the harbor. Next to it stood the smaller gallows where ordinary criminals like Manuel were executed. Manuel's wife, holding their infant son in her arms, stood as close to it as was allowed, as did several of his friends from the slave house, who were prepared to rush forward and pull on his legs if need be to shorten his suffering.

When Manuel was led out, his hands tied in front of him so he could still lift them in prayer, the crowd gasped at his huge size. Standing next to little fellows like Dominee Bogardus and Meester Hans, he looked mountainous. Director Kieft pronounced sentence. Evert prayed for the soul of the murdered man, for the soul of the man about to die, for the wisdom of those who govern this community, and for all those who live within it. The executioner, also African, helped Manuel climb to the spot from which he must step into oblivion. Taking no chances, his friend and killer put two ropes around Manuel's neck and then, after Manuel nodded that he was ready, pushed him from the ladder. Manuel fell . . . and both ropes broke.

Meester Hans rushed to the fallen man, loosening the ropes from his neck and feeling for a pulse. "He lives!"

Tymen, standing near the front of the crowd, took up the cry: "He lives!" Marritje, grasping his arm, went further: "It's the Will of God!" People were crying and praying, several fainted, and all agreed: Manuel was innocent.

Director Kieft was frustrated. He wanted someone to die this day, but clearly it was not going to be Manuel. He grudgingly granted a pardon and let the crowd get on with its celebrating, which continued through the night and into the next day.

Evert, who normally preferred to be out in the world comforting the sick and dying, converting the heathen, and admonishing the wicked, chose to take the rest of the day off. He puttered around the parsonage all afternoon, humming one of the less lugubrious psalms. When Anneke looked at him questioningly, he winked and said, "I just love a good miracle, don't you?"

Well, yes, she supposed that she did. "You didn't have anything to do with that particular miracle, did you?"

"Me? Never! I just explained to the executioner that killing is a great sin that no man would want to have on his conscience."

"Anything else?"

"No, nothing. Except I gave him three guilders for a job well done."

Five

KIEFT'S WAR

(1640–1643)

New Amsterdam

Anneke frowned when she saw Govert Loockermans at the parsonage door. She knew that Evert was fond of the boy, but there was a recklessness about him that made her uneasy. Cornelis van Tienhoven had led a raid on the Raritan yesterday, and the things she had heard about Govert's brutal behavior there troubled her.

"I need to see the dominee," Govert said.

"He's not home."

"I can wait on the stoop."

Anneke sighed and unlatched the bottom half of the door. "You wait here," she said pointing to a chair. "I have work to do."

Too restless to sit, Govert paced the small front room of the parsonage, occasionally glowering at the massive Bible that dominated the table by the window. *Everything was so damnably unfair!* Here he was, only just turned twenty-two! He had just finished his contract with the WIC and scraped together enough money to lease the river sloop *Wesel* from Maryn Adriaensen. He had also just signed his first contract to purchase maize from the Wilden and was finally set to make his first fortune, and now, just because he had risked his life to protect the colony, no one would speak to him except Evert, and Evert would talk to anyone.

Evert's friendship with Govert had begun aboard the *Zoutberg*, the ship that brought them both to the New World. Govert, who was tall and muscular and looked at the time to be about eighteen, had joined the crew as cook's mate, but during the hours of shipboard tedium, he confided to Evert that he was only fifteen, a refugee from war-torn Spanish Netherland. Evert had assumed the boy was fleeing religious persecution, but Govert corrected him, saying, "No, Dominee, I was fleeing Spanish soldiers. I didn't want to be conscripted."

Govert didn't have much use for the Dutch Reformed Church or for Evert's sermons either, but ever since their journey together he had made a point of stopping by from time to time to talk to the older man—generally when he was worried about something. And Evert still had a soft spot for the boy who ran away from home at age fifteen to reinvent himself. Govert would always be welcome at the parsonage.

When Evert finally arrived, he could tell from Govert's scowl there was going to be a difficult conversation ahead. He fetched some weak beer and pipes and sat down to listen. The Church didn't hold with confession, but Evert still found the simple act of talking was often enough to relieve a troubled soul.

"What happened?" Evert knew, but he wanted Govert to tell him.

"A bunch of Raritan attacked one of our sloops, and then they stole some hogs from the De Vries plantation."

"David de Vries says Dutch men took his hogs."

"Well, we *thought* the Raritan took them. Director Kieft wanted to make an example of them, so he told Van Tienhoven to take some of our men and show them we won't tolerate their insolence."

Evert nodded. Everyone knew that Director Kieft had no idea how to conduct himself with the Wilden. Last year, he had wanted to tax them for "providing protection." When they stopped laughing, they refused, so now he wanted to impress them with displays of force, and Secretary Van Tienhoven only egged him on.

"There were about seventy of us," Govert continued, "WIC soldiers and volunteers and some of the sailors from that ship in harbor. I took about fifteen of the sailors with me on the *Wesel*, and we knew what we needed to do."

"What was that?"

"To kill the savages."

"Were those your orders?"

"Not exactly, but Van Tienhoven said if they refused to pay for the hogs, we should ruin their crops and take prisoners, but then he said he was going to leave and he expected all of us who remained to defend our just cause, so it was pretty clear what he wanted."

"Did *you* behave in a savage manner?"

"I was angry. I took the brother of the sachem and tied him to the mast of the *Wesel*."

"And then?"

Govert looked up angrily. "I took a splintered plank and rammed it into his balls."

Evert winced, but then he asked, "Are you sorry?"

Govert was still defiant. "I'm sorry everyone is making such a fuss. We were supposed to make an example of them, and we did."

"Would you do it again?"

"Maybe. Probably not. I don't know."

Evert sighed. He felt responsible for this wayward youth, and this was as close to repentance as they were ever going to get. The next hurdle, he knew, would be bringing the boy back into the community. "Anneke," he yelled, "grab your cloak. We're going out for dinner."

When they arrived at the *Stadsherberg*, proprietor Philip Gerritsen took one look at Govert's glowering face and immediately offered them a private room.

"Oh, no!" Evert waved the offer away. "The City Tavern is a place to see and be seen. Give us a table in the front room, and if anyone else would care to join us, I'll foot the bill."

As they sat in awkward silence, Anneke nervously fingered the stem of her *roemer*, wondering how large that bill was going to be.

Soon Marritje showed up with Tymen in tow. "What are we celebrating?" she whispered to Anneke.

"Prodigal Son," came the whispered reply.

Marritje made a point of sitting next to Govert. *Sure, everyone was calling him a murderer, but he was a good-looking kid and always fun to talk to*. Then she turned back to Anneke and said, "You know, your Jan follows Tymen around like a puppy. He's old enough now to start an apprenticeship. Why don't you send him to live with us and learn to be a carpenter?"

Anneke looked questioningly at Evert even though she knew that he would leave any decision regarding Roelof's children to her.

Barent Jacobsen and his father-in-law Leendert Arentsen joined the party. Both of them had been seamen on the *Dolphyn* before settling in the colony. "Say! that *Dolphyn* was some leaky vessel," Tymen greeted them. "You guys were lucky to get here at all."

"You don't know the half of it," Leendert exclaimed. "That ship was leaking so much that all of us crewmen refused to sail. Finally, the schipper poached a carpenter from the *Haring*."

"But by then," Barent chimed in, "so much of the food had already gone bad that some of the passengers only got half rations. Jan Schepmoes and his family would have starved if we hadn't helped them out."

Round and rosy Hendrick Jansen turned up with a basket of fresh pretzels. "Can't let 'em go stale!" He announced plans to marry Femmetje Alberts, the tall and angular niece of Barent Dircksen van Norden.

"A baking dynasty," Marritje cheered. Then she whispered to her sister, "And won't they be a sight together!"

Storytelling is thirsty work, so Evert called for another round.

"Bonjour!" Christine trilled from the doorway, coming in with a livid bruise on her face.

All eyes turned to Dirck Holgertsen, who bellowed, "Not me!" while pointing to the abrasions on his own face. "That miserable miser who married her mother threw her off the stoop of her own house." Everyone groaned in sympathy. They all knew Christine's stepfather, Jan Jansen Damen, was the meanest man in town.

"We were at Jan Jansen's house," Dirck said, "which by rights ought to be Christine's. The old codfish said I owed him three guilders, which is *not* true, and when I refused to pay, he yelled, 'Begone out of the house,' and he *threw* Christine down the stairs. And *then* he came at her with a knife!"

Christine proudly displayed the rent in her skirt as evidence. "And Dirck threw a pewter can at him to make him stop, and then Jan Jansen shouted, 'If you have the courage, draw your knife,' and he went after Dirck, but Dirck, thank Heaven, was sober at the time, so he only hit him with a post, and no one got killed."

By the end of the evening, people were too caught up in their own dramas to pay any attention to Govert. Evert needed a little help walking home, which Govert was happy to provide. Just before they reached the parsonage, he said, "Thank you, Pater."

Evert, almost sober, responded, "Go in peace, my son."

Amsterdam

Five months later found Govert sitting in a seamen's hostel in Amsterdam slurping herring down headfirst and chasing them with hoppy Dutch beer. He looked like a sailor in his long coat and sailcloth breeches for the simple reason that he had just paid his passage home by working crew. He planned to save money his first night in town by sharing a room with three of his shipmates, but becoming a common seaman did not fit into the rest of his plans.

The next morning, Govert sought out one of the many barber-surgeons who operated along the waterfront and invested in a shave and a haircut. Wearing a clean linen shirt under his dusty doublet, he made his way along the Brouwersgracht to the West-Indisch Huis, the former meat market that the WIC had rented as headquarters for its overseas empire. When Govert had last seen Amsterdam seven years ago, he had been too frightened and alone to take much in, but today he reveled in the chaos of the place. *The Dutch*, he thought, *were truly masters of land and sea*. The city was being expanded with rings of new canals lined with ostentatiously ornate merchants' homes. The streets thronged with prune-faced

Puritans, scintillating Sephardim, moody Muscovites, and riffraff from every corner of the earth, and Govert longed to be a part of it.

As Govert had hoped, he found his old boss, Wouter van Twiller, at the West-Indisch Huis. Wouter, eager for gossip, was genuinely pleased to see a familiar face. "Tell me," he asked, "how do you feel about Arabic wine? Do you have a favorite koffiehuis?"

"Oh, well, naturally," Govert bluffed, "but I'm sure that any place that you suggest will be splendid."

"How about the Polish House on Kalverstraat near the Stock Exchange. What say we meet there around four o'clock?"

Govert made a point of seeking out the Polish House early and waiting discreetly outside until he saw Wouter approach. Entering the unfamiliar establishment, Govert saw gentlemen sitting in groups of two or three, some in wigs and some with their heads uncovered, reading newspapers or playing trictrac and talking, seemingly all at the same time. A woman in a starched apron and cap stood behind a counter ready to serve them, and a small boy of about eight skipped around from table to table handing out pipes and taking away empty dishes. Most noticeable, though, were an acrid burning smell and a rattling noise.

"They roast 'em first, you know, before they grind them into powder," Wouter observed, selecting a corner table away from the trictrac players and signaling for two pipes and two bowls.

The serving boy promptly brought them pipes and a brazier of coals for lighting them. A moment later the matron set two red earthenware bowls filled with steaming black sludge in front of them. Determined not to betray his inexperience, Govert waited for Wouter to take a first sip and then copied his movements. A nasty taste filled his mouth, and he fought back a grimace, but when Wouter took a second sip, so did Govert. Suddenly he felt flushed, and his pulse quickened.

"This stuff is . . . intoxicating," he said.

"Isn't it just?" Wouter agreed, leaning back in his chair. "The man who can figure out how to import koffie to the New World will make a fortune. Now tell me, Govert, how have things been since I left? How's Willem Kieft getting along?"

Without mentioning his own role in the recent fracas, Govert told Wouter about the increasing tensions with the Wilden and the fear that all of the farmsteads south of Fort Orange might soon need to be abandoned.

Wouter seemed gratified to hear that his successor was so roundly disliked. He puffed on his pipe a few more times staring absently across the smoke-filled room and then turned back to Govert and said self-importantly, "And now, tell me what I can do for you."

"I have two trunks of beaver pelts back at my lodging."

"My, my," Wouter said, "the Company relinquished its monopoly on fur just last year, and here a young fellow like you is already ready to trade. As soon as we finish up here, we'll go back to the WIC. They'll buy everything you have."

"I need clothing."

Wouter nodded. "I'll give you the address of my tailor. Tell him I sent you, and he'll give you a fair price. And Govert, don't tell him what you want. Let him tell you what you need. And stay away from bright colors. Can't have you looking like a Catholic."

"No, indeed," Govert agreed. "I hope to look like a prosperous merchant. I've learned pretty much everything there is to know about trade in the New World, but I am unable to invest as I would like. I am hoping to find a partner."

"Ah, that is going to be a little bit trickier. The prominent trading firms prefer to keep everything in the family."

Govert smiled disarmingly. "I'm available."

Wouter hesitated. "Does the name Verbrugge mean anything to you?"

"Of course, it does," Govert lied.

"They have some experience in international trade and are hoping to expand. And Gillis Verbrugge has a recently widowed niece . . ."

The wedding took place in the stylish Westerkerk, conveniently located on the Prinsengracht near to the WIC offices and to the home of Seth Verbrugge, where Govert had been staying ever since his return from visiting his family in Turnhout. His father dead, the family home sold to pay debts, the effects of war everywhere—Govert hoped never to see the place again. His favorite sister, Annette, came back with him to Amsterdam. With all of the young men in Turnhout crippled or dead, her prospects there were dismal. "Come with me," he urged. "I'll make you the richest woman in the New World."

The whitewashed walls of the church seemed a little plain to Govert, but the towering vault of the nave was certainly impressive, quite a contrast to the rickety church where Evert conducted services. Govert had followed Wouter's advice and stayed away from the rich scarlet and gold cloths that had at first caught his eye, but he thought he looked quite handsome in his new mulberry doublet and fashionably flat lace collar, and his dearest acquisition, a broad-brimmed hat of felted beaver, marked him, in his opinion, as a gentleman of substance.

While waiting for the dominee, Govert looked appraisingly at his bride. With her sallow complexion and long nose, she didn't look very robust, but, Govert thought, you couldn't fault her for courage. Everyone knew the story of her first marriage to Captain Jan van de Water. He went to sea shortly before their son Hendrick was born, and Adriantje didn't learn of his death in a hurricane until *after* she had sailed to join him in New Amsterdam. She could've stayed on—plenty of men looking for wives in the New World—but she chose to return to her family in Haarlem, and now here she was—getting ready to cross the ocean once again. He glanced at her one more time and decided her face didn't matter. Her richly brocaded stomacher and cuffs and the extravagant lace points on her cap marked her as his portal to a new life.

And Adriantje, her eyes cast demurely downward, covertly took stock of her groom. She wasn't entirely displeased. True, a company clerk was not nearly as exciting as a ship's captain, but Govert looked quite presentable in his new suit of clothes, and she knew that just as soon as this transaction was complete, he would step into his role as New World factor for the Verbrugge Trading Firm. She understood perfectly well that she was a pawn in the family business, but she hoped that in the great game of global trade she someday might be crowned a queen.

New Amsterdam

While Govert was away changing his fortune in the Old World, clashes with the Wilden continued to mount in the colony.

Tryn stopped by the parsonage to check on Anneke and the boys and to share the latest news. Willem, named for Evert's father, had always been an easy child, but Cornelis, named for Evert's brother, tended to be sickly. "They're too close in age," Tryn said, pouring herself a glass of weak beer. "Having children just a year apart is hard on the mother and on the children."

Anneke, concentrating on pouring flour into her bolting box, made no response, so Tryn continued, "Do you remember Claes Swits?"

"The wheelwright? Of course, I do."

"He's dead."

Anneke looked up in alarm. She had seen Claes just a couple of days ago at church, and he seemed perfectly healthy then.

"Murdered, in fact."

"That sweet old man! Who would do such a thing?"

"One of the Wecquaesgeeks. People say that years ago when the killer was a child, he saw three white men murder his uncle, and he swore someday to take revenge. Yesterday, he stopped by Claes's cabin to trade, but when Claes bent over to take some duffle out of his trunk, the scoundrel picked up an axe and whacked off his head."

"How could anyone possibly know such a thing?" Anneke exclaimed. "Has the murderer confessed?"

Tryn shrugged. She wasn't about to let facts get in the way of a good story. "He hasn't been caught yet. They're having a big meeting up at the fort right now trying to decide what to do."

Evert came home late that afternoon looking tired and gray. He kissed his wife and tossed each of his boys into the air: "Hoi, Willem Evertsen! Hoi, Cornelis Evertsen!" *It was grand to be the father of sons.*

"Tryn told me Claes Swits has been murdered. Will this mean war?" Anneke asked.

"That's what Kieft would like. He wants to treat the Wilden like unruly serfs who can be forced into submission, but he doesn't want to be held responsible, so he's done a very clever thing: He's appointed a group of twelve freemen to advise him. He expects them to approve everything he does, but then if things go wrong, it will be their fault and not his."

"Who's in this group?"

"Well, as you'd expect, they're all landowners, but most of them are God-fearing people who will not let themselves be pushed into unnecessary violence. The Chair is David de Vries."

"The one whose hogs were stolen?"

"Yeah, and *not* by the Raritan. He's a patroon, so he has a lot invested in the colony. And he's already lost a lot—the Raritan retaliated for the last raid by burning his tobacco barn and killing four of his tenants—but he still has a lot more to lose. He also knows the Indians better than anyone else. He keeps saying they're as vengeful as Italians. He means it as a warning, but since no one knows what he's talking about, it goes unheeded."

"Anyone else?"

"Maryn Adriaensen."

"Oh, no! I've known Maryn almost as long as I've lived here. He's a *terrible* bully, and he thinks every problem can be solved with a gun."

"And Jan Jansen Damen and his son-in-law, Abraham Verplanck."

"Even worse! Those two think the Natives are vermin."

"They're the worst ones. Everyone else seems sensible. Jochim Kuyter will be a good influence."

"The Dane?"

"Yes. He's educated and devout, and he also has quite a bit of property that he will want to protect."

"And what exactly are these fellows supposed to do?"

"Determine whether it is just to punish the murderer of Claes Swits, and in the case that the Indians refuse to surrender the murderer, decide whether it is justifiable to ruin the entire village to which he belongs."

Anneke kept Jan's head firmly pinned between her knees while combing the nits out of his hair. They were interrupted by Tryn, who had been out all night assisting at a delivery. Anneke could tell from the look on her mother's face that the news was not good, but she asked anyway, "How'd it go?"

Tryn dropped down exhausted on a stool, and Jan escaped. "It was a boy, but we lost both of them." She gratefully accepted a glass of weak beer and sat for a moment with her eyes closed, but then she looked up and said, "I've found a husband for Sara."

"Oh, no, Mamma! She's too young. She's only fifteen."

"She's been a woman for over a year now, and she'll marry soon whether you like it or not. The least we can do is help her find a decent man so she doesn't go running off with a Wilt."

Anneke smiled at her mother's exaggeration, but she also knew there was some truth to what she said. Just last year, Sara had stopped attending school because Meester Adam had been paying attention to her in ways that made her uncomfortable.

"Who did you have in mind?"

"Hans Kierstede."

"Oh, no, Mamma! He's too old. He's thirty if he's a day. He's *German*."

"Well, at least he's *Lutheran*," Tryn snapped. But then she continued in a more conciliatory tone. "Marry your daughters well, Anneke. I spent last night watching Meester Hans trying to save the life of a young mother. He is a healer and a teacher. He will take care of Sara, and as his wife, she will be one of the most respected women in the colony. You cannot ask for more."

Anneke nodded slowly. "Talk to him."

Anneke had never expected to cry at her daughter's wedding, but when she saw Sara give her small hand to Meester Hans and heard Evert pronounce them man and wife, she burst into tears. Tryn, wiping away a tear of her own, squeezed her hand and said, "There, there! It's a joyous day."

After the solemn church service, everyone was happy to retreat to the parsonage to celebrate. Hippocras, the spiced wine known as Bride's Tears, flowed in rivers, and for this happy occasion Evert had also commissioned a special *trouwbier* from Lubbert the Brewer. Hans at first seemed to find the rowdy humor unsettling, but then he relaxed and joined in the fun. Sara tried to stay as close to her mother as possible until at last Anneke said, "You're a married woman now. Go greet your guests, laugh at their bawdy jokes, and act like you appreciate every single bit of advice they give you."

Tryn was gratified to see how many of the prominent members of the community had turned out, but then, they would, wouldn't they, for the marriage of the dominee's stepdaughter. Laughing, talking, eating, and drinking all at once, the crowd spilled out of the parsonage into the orchard, where a fiddler, his long instrument held in the crook of his arm, played for the circling dancers.

Govert, who had returned to the colony late last year, came alone, saying his wife Adriantje was suffering from a sick headache. Tymen questioned him about his latest yacht, while Hans's brother Jochem, who walked with a limp and was normally so shy, chatted happily with Marritje. Govert's sister Annette, who looked so much like her brother with her high cheekbones and darting eyes, was radiant in a gown of dark maroon, clearly delighted to be seen in public with her new husband Olof van Cortlandt, already a rising star in the colony and the righthand man of Director Kieft. Meester

Adam backed Katryn into a corner, but Anneke quickly intervened. Girls needed an education, but not the kind that he had in mind. And Director Kieft was there also, huddled in the hallway with Evert and whispering in a way that made Anneke nervous. Those two never saw eye to eye.

Glasses were raised to the young couple, to their parents, to their future children. "Tell me, David Pietersen," Evert said loudly to David de Vries, "You've traveled a lot. What can you tell us about the settlements of the English up north."

"Well," said De Vries, who was in on the plot, "they're pretty well run. Each settlement begins by building a church—small but tidy, a testament to their piety."

"Do you hear that?" Evert thundered. "What a pity we have no such piety. I have even heard English guests liken our own church to a mean wooden barn."

Kieft appeared stung. "This cannot stand! I will personally pledge forty guilders to build a new *stone* church inside the fort."

Govert was feeling exceptionally generous that day. "I'll match your forty!"

Olof van Cortlandt glanced over his shoulder at his brother-in-law and said, "I can afford sixty."

Kieft told Van Tienhoven to take notes.

Maryn Adriaensen volunteered four beaver.

Dirck Holgertsen pledged fifteen strings of sewant.

Hendrick the Baker promised twenty schepels of wheat.

Jan Jansen Damen, who was a church warden, offered one hundred guilders.

By the end of the evening, one thousand eight hundred guilders had been pledged. Every stiver would be collected.

On a cold Shrove Tuesday in February, something frightening was happening across the river. The snow was still deep on the ground, but Indians had started arriving in large numbers—dozens at first and then hundreds. Evert went to the fort to find out what was going on, but he came back again without much to report.

"It's not a war party," he reassured Anneke, "but no one at the fort is quite sure what it is. Some people say it's Tappan, but others say Wecquaesgeek. There seem to be a lot of women and children with them. Many of them are injured, and they're not dressed for the cold. It's possible they've been attacked—maybe by Mohawks, maybe by Mohicans—and they're coming to us for protection."

"Why would they come to us?" she asked.

"I'm not sure. I think when we bought this land from them, they may have thought we meant to enter into a mutual protection alliance."

The unsettling news of Indians congregating on the other side of the river did little to dampen the Shrove Tuesday celebrations that were already underway. Evert condemned *Vastenavond* as a Romish superstition left over from the days of Bacchus, but he was always happy to enjoy pancakes dripping with butter and to show off his remarkably talented sons in good company, so Anneke invited Sara and Hans and Hans's brother Jochem for a family dinner.

Outside, they could hear carousing youths who, despite repeated prohibitions, had dressed themselves in women's skirts and caps and gotten up a game of *ganstrekken*. The object of their game was to capture a prize goose that had been greased and suspended by its feet from the branch of a massive oak tree down by the fort. The boys would ride by at full tilt, attempting to grab the luckless animal by its neck and pull it free, but more often they were the ones who fell to the ground provoking jeers and laughter.

Anneke sat by the hearth ladling batter into her long-handled pancake pan. Hearing a loud shriek, she said to Hans, "You'll have a number of new patients tonight."

"That I will," Hans agreed, "and most of them victims of their own stupidity."

Jan Jansen Damen was also hosting a family dinner on that Shrove Tuesday. He did not invite his stepdaughter Christine, but he did invite her sisters Maria and Rachel and their respective husbands: Abraham Verplank and Cornelis van Tienhoven. To round out his guest list, he had also included Maryn Adriaensen with his wife Lysbet. Their guest of honor, of course, was Willem Kieft.

The party began well enough with baked oysters, and then they moved on to turkey stewed with sorrel. Soon the talk turned to the Wilden, and Kieft fumed with impotence: "How I would love to shove a bit in their mouth!"

Van Tienhoven handed him a petition. "What would you think of this?"

Kieft read that the undersigned members of the Twelve Men wished to be avenged on the savages whom God had evidently given into our hands. Kieft nodded slowly. This would do very nicely, very nicely indeed.

The next day, as they walked to the fort for the Ash Wednesday sermon, Anneke wondered whether Evert ever regretted the part he had played in raising funds to build the new church. It was a handsome building. Designed and built by English carpenters, it had oaken shingles that gleamed like slate and a tall bell tower with a sundial on one side. It was a building to be proud of, but the decision to place it inside the fort marked it as WIC property, and many were uncomfortable worshiping there.

Evert excelled at urging people to repent, but Anneke thought his sermons sometimes were a bit tedious. Instead of calling on his congregation to renounce lust, envy, gluttony, and sloth, why not just ask them to give up being human and be done with it? Today, though, his remarks seemed quite pointed. "We are still in the darkness of sin, but if we examine our beliefs and behavior, we yet may emerge into the light of the Resurrection. Let us welcome the refugee at our gates, feed the hungry, and care for the injured and sick." And then, just for good measure, let us also give up pride, greed, and wrath . . . especially pride, greed, and wrath.

As the shadows grew long on that snowy Ash Wednesday, Jochem came to the door of the parsonage and asked for Evert. Anneke invited him into the front room and went out back to call her husband in from the orchard, where he had been trying to teach four-year-old Willem how to play *kolf*.

Evert galloped in with young Willem riding on his shoulders. "That boy's going to break windows someday! You ought to see him smack that ball," he said proudly.

"Evert," Jochem said quietly, "something bad's going on at the fort. I think you need to be there."

"What's happening?" Evert asked, taking Willem down and handing him to Anneke.

"The WIC soldiers are preparing to go out on a raid tonight, and a lot of the colonists are joining them. They mean to attack the Wilden at midnight."

"They can't do that," Anneke cried. "They'll all be sleeping!"

Evert put his arm around her and held her close. They could, and they would.

"Evert," Jochem repeated, "I think you may need to be away for a long time. I want to stay here with Anneke and the children . . . just in case."

"Oh, that's not necessary," Anneke protested. "We've never been afraid of Wilden."

"It's not my idea," Jochem said. "Sara asked me to stay with you, and I mean to stay."

Toward midnight, the firing began, and Anneke listened to the shrieks and the moans of the dying throughout the night. She nursed Baby Jonas, swaddled him, and returned him to his cradle, and then she tried to sleep herself, but she woke up screaming, after dreaming that Kitpul was about to split her skull with her old heavy knife. She tried again to sleep but woke up sobbing, having dreamt that she saw Welanie lying dead in the snow, shot through the breast by a vengeful colonist. At last she gave up and climbed down from her bed and went into the back room, where she found Jochem sitting with a cold pipe by the banked fire of the hearth staring into the darkness.

When he heard her approach, he looked up and said, "Magdeburg."

Anneke bent down to stir up the fire and then pulled over a stool and sat down beside him. She knew both of the brothers came from Magdeburg, but otherwise the name meant nothing to her. "What about it?" she asked.

"Magdeburg was the grandest and most beautiful city in all of Europe," he began.

"What happened?"

"The emperor decided that Magdeburg should become Catholic again. We were very much opposed and thought the Swedes would help us, but they didn't."

"Were you there?"

Jochem nodded. "Our parents had a middle-sized holding. We had an older sister, Gertrud, and two younger brothers. Germans usually give all children equal inheritance, but they knew that dividing such a small place among the five of us would be ruinous, so they decided I would keep the farm and Hans, the brainy one, would apprentice as a surgeon. Later they would give Gertrud a dowry of equal value, and either they or I would arrange similar apprenticeships for the younger boys. When the siege started in 1631, Hans had just finished his apprenticeship and begun his Wanderjahr."

Anneke looked at him questioningly.

"You know, when journeymen leave home and work for different masters to broaden their experience. He was in Schönebeck when the siege started. It lasted two months, and then they decided to storm the walls. I went to the ramparts with my father and brothers even though they were just little kids. I was shot early on when people still thought they could save something. Someone dragged me to the cathedral. When they breached the walls, the entire army surged in—there were almost twice as many of them as there were of us—and started burning and looting. We used to be a huge city—more than twenty thousand people lived there—but when it was over, there were scarcely a thousand of us left, and that's only because they decided to save our beautiful cathedral for Catholicism. One of the men who raped Gertrud took her back to camp with him." He laughed bitterly. "It's called a Magdeburg Marriage. I never saw her again."

"How did you survive?"

"Hans came back and found me. Any other surgeon would have amputated this leg, but he found a cart and dragged me back to Schönebeck. Instead of cauterizing my wound with boiling oil, he washed it with wine—said it's the modern method—set the bone and stitched the flesh back together and then covered it all with a salve he made from egg and honey. When I could travel again, we found the Swedish army and both signed up. Surgeons are always needed, and I was able to work in the baggage train. After a time, we heard a rumor that the WIC was looking for surgeons to send to the New World. We figured any world would be better than the one we were in, so Hans applied."

"And you never married . . ."

He looked at her in surprise. "Why would you say that? My Lotte was the smartest, kindest woman in Christendom. We had two sturdy sons, Adam and Michael, and our Tilde was the most beautiful angel you ever saw."

He looked back into the darkness. "All gone."

Indians who knew the parsonage as a place of refuge started arriving predawn. They thought they had been attacked by Mohawks. Anneke treated their wounds while explaining as best she could that the people to whom they had come for protection were the ones who had harmed them. She gave them food and told them they must go and warn the others to stay away.

Evert returned sick with anger and grief. It was true that his efforts to convert the heathen had not been very successful to date, but he felt spiritually responsible for *all* of the inhabitants of this strange world, and now large numbers of innocents—some said as many as a hundred and twenty—had been ruthlessly slaughtered in their sleep.

David de Vries was furious. *He* was still the chair of the Twelve Men, and this action never should have been undertaken without his approval. He and every other colonist living outside the immediate vicinity of the fort would lose everything. He promised that he would interview every survivor he could find and discover how this atrocity was perpetrated.

Bit by bit the details came out. The infamous request to attack was signed by three men— Jan Damen, Abraham Verplanck, and Maryn Adriaensen—*on behalf of the Twelve*. Van

Tienhoven took the main force across the river to deal with the larger body of refugees while Maryn Adriaensen took on a smaller group of Wecquaesgeeks at Corlaer's Hook. Govert Loockermans was his second-in-command.

Rumors swirled. They couldn't all be true, but they all emphasized the inhumanity of what had happened:

The very young and the very old were thrown into the river to drown.

Infants were hacked to pieces in their cradle boards.

Corpses were mutilated.

Captives had been tortured and killed.

And Kieft shook the hand of every man who returned.

Anneke looked angrily at Evert. There would be no forgiveness for Govert this time around.

A COMMUNITY DIVIDED

(1643–1645)

New Amsterdam

The midnight massacre united the tribes of the Algonquian in a single purpose: driving the Swanneken back into the sea. As Evert had predicted, Kieft lay the blame for the catastrophe at the feet of the Twelve. His defense was truly stunning. He justified his actions, saying: "The savages were suspected of intending a general massacre, but God would not suffer such wickedness to go on for any length of time. He awakened the community to justice and the revenge for Christian blood. With this resolve some deputies in the name of all submitted a request to be allowed to carry out the revenge . . ."

And as David de Vries had predicted, the surrounding farmsteads were all devastated, but here, too, Kieft was blameless. He explained: "Fearing to bring trouble over the land, we set before our deputies the difficult situation, especially of the houses far out in the country and inhabited by only a few people, which it would be necessary to abandon, as we had no forces to garrison them all with soldiers, but they made their request so urgently, saying, 'If we would not consent, the blood would be on our heads,' that we were compelled to give our consent and to assist them with our soldiers . . ."

Farmsteads were burnt, livestock slaughtered, men killed, and women and children taken captive. The greatest danger, though, was not that Kieft had united the Algonquian, but that he had divided the Dutch. Neighbor reviled neighbor, brother would not speak to brother, mothers hated their daughters, and sons turned against their fathers. Evert was in despair.

Maryn Adriaensen sat in the City Tavern nursing a pint and a grievance. He couldn't stand the opprobrium. "It's not fair," he said to his wife, Lysbet. "I've lost just as much as the next man." The official record stated that the attack was undertaken at *his* request. *Well, maybe he did request it, but that was no reason to blame him for everything.*

Dirck Holgertsen walked past without greeting him. From the next room Maryn heard, or thought he heard, someone say, "Murderer." He slammed his fist on the table, jumped up from his seat, and rushed from the room, leaving Lysbet sitting in bewilderment. At last, one of her neighbors asked her what was wrong.

"My man means to kill the director. Go and catch him!"

Maryn by that time had reached the fort. Brandishing a sword and a loaded pistol, he rushed through the door of Kieft's house and into his office. Pointing his cocked pistol at Kieft, he yelled, "What devilish lies have you been telling about me?" Councilman Johannes la Montagne happened to be standing close enough to intervene. As Maryn lowered the match cord and prepared to fire, La Montagne stuck his thumb between the match and the powder pan. At the expense of a burned thumb, catastrophe was averted. Hearing the commotion, guards came running to arrest Maryn and take him away.

Anneke was scrubbing the front stoop of the parsonage when she heard shots coming from the fort—two in rapid succession followed by a third. Alarmed, she called for Katryn to finish the scrubbing while she went to investigate.

At the fort, she found a crowd of about thirty people with Evert at their head demanding Maryn's release. When Kieft turned and slammed the door on their demands, Jacob Stangh fired two shots after him, prompting the sentry to shoot Jacob dead. His head would be displayed as a warning to others who would make attempts on the lives of their God-given leaders.

Evert didn't like Maryn. He didn't like the way the man annoyed Anneke after Roelof died, and he certainly didn't like the role he had played in bringing warfare upon the colony, but he knew that Kieft had no judicial power in this situation. The people assembled here today wanted a semblance of legality, not a one-man tribunal. Kieft, ever decisive, said that he would leave the matter to their conscience.

"Choose a council of eight men," Evert instructed them. "Let them deliberate and decide." Eight men were quickly selected, and after a brief discussion, they pronounced sentence: Maryn would be set free on the condition that he pay a fine of five hundred guilders and stay away from Manhattan for three months.

Kieft, who had been expecting something more along the lines of "hang by the neck until dead," would not countenance the colonists' clemency. In the end, he decreed that Maryn be sent back to Patria for judgment. It was not the outcome Evert had hoped for but one that he had to accept.

As Anneke turned to leave, she recognized Jochem limping across the parade ground toward her. Since the night of the massacre, he had become a frequent guest at the parsonage. Anneke waited for him to catch up with her and then turned and set off toward her own house, knowing Jochem would accompany her.

"That man of yours sure likes to be in the thick of things," he greeted her.

"That he does," she agreed. "I'll never need to worry about being bored as long as I'm married to Evert."

"I've been collecting winter clothes for the refugees. Should I bring them by the parsonage this evening?" Jochem asked.

"No, the old church is a better distribution point. Leave the clothing there, but then stop by and sup with us, heh?"

As they turned the corner onto Anneke's street, they could see Katryn emptying her washbasin by the now clean stoop.

"You'll be wanting a wife, Jochem," Anneke said, following some unspoken logic. "My Katryn's a fine girl. You could do worse."

Jochem looked at her in surprise. "I don't want any of your girls, Anna Jans." Then he laughed and said, "Oh, don't look so hurt. I don't want anyone's *girl.* Hans and Sara get along fine, but I'm too old to take on a teenager. I need a partner in life, a woman of kindness and judgment. And if I can't have that, I'll live out my days alone."

That night, Anneke permitted herself a rare moment of vanity. Could Jochem have been thinking of her? But she quickly dismissed the idea. Here she was—an old woman of thirty-eight, the mother of eight with her first grandchild already on the way. It was unlikely that any man would ever look upon her as anything but a *predikantsvrouw* ever again.

In the days that followed, as refugees poured in from the outlying farmsteads, the parsonage became a popular meeting place, especially among those who felt the crisis they were enduring had been brought upon them by their own leaders. Hans and Jochem were both there the day Evert came in shaking his head. "He's done it again," he said. "Kieft's appointed another advisory council—this time a group of eight."

"Why eight?" Anneke asked.

"Dunno. Maybe eight are easier to control. Maybe he could only find eight men willing to work with him."

"Who will chair it now that David de Vries has gone back to Patria?" Jochem asked.

"Cornelis Melyn. He's been here about four years now, has a patroonship on Staten Island. I think he'll be good."

"Is there anyone else we know?"

"Well, Jochim Kuyter is back. And here's an interesting thing—Kieft has included two Englishmen: Thomas Hall and Isaac Allerton."

"That makes sense," Hans said. "He needs to assure that the English will stand with us against the Indians if we need help."

"We're already at war," Anneke said. "What else can he want them to approve?"

"He needs to raise money. The fort is in poor repair, and he only has about forty-five soldiers. He wants them to approve new taxes . . ."

"On what?"

"On beaver . . ."

"That'll never work," Jochem said.

". . . and beer."

"He can't do that to starving people! He doesn't have the right," Anneke exclaimed.

"That's what the Eight Men told him, but he answered that in this country he is his own master and may do as he pleases. And Philip Gerritsen has already been arrested for refusing to pay."

As the violence continued, settlers abandoned their ruined farmsteads and flocked to Manhattan hoping to find protection there. Almost every household in New Amsterdam was now sheltering refugees, and people who could not find housing were living in makeshift tents alongside the fort. Anneke and Evert took in Hans Jansen, a landowner from Long Island, with his wife Reymerig and their five children. Hans Jansen talked incessantly about the damage done to their farmstead and their lost livestock and crops, but Reymerig, tall and gaunt, her once red hair now graying, sat quietly and said very little. Anneke knew that the family had lost a sixth child, a little girl, just before the Indian attacks, and Reymerig still seemed lost in her grief.

Hans Jansen and Reymerig had been farming on Long Island since 1639, but, they told their hosts, they originally came from Noordstrand.

"Noordstrand . . ." Evert said thoughtfully. "Isn't that the island where they had such a terrible storm?"

"The same," Hans Jansen answered. "The whole island was pretty much destroyed, and we lost everything we owned. Anyone who lives on an island is used to storms, but the storm of 1634 was worse than anyone living could ever imagine. The wind raged for hours, and finally the storm surge broke the dikes and swallowed the island."

"How did you save yourselves?" Anneke asked.

"We ran to the church in Odenbüll and sheltered there. When the waters subsided, we could see that most of our island had vanished. More than half of the villagers drowned. We found the bodies of my brother and two of his children, but everyone else had washed away."

"We were just lucky," Reymerig said. "We stayed with some of my family inland for a while, but then we learned that farmers were wanted here, so we came. And now it's happening all over again."

"No, it isn't, Reymetje," her husband comforted her. "Nothing can ever take the land away from us here. We'll go back and build everything again."

Anneke and Reymerig shared the box bed closest to the hearth while everyone else slept in the loft or on the floor. After they drew the curtains shut for warmth and privacy, Reymerig would weep, and Anneke didn't know how to comfort her, so at last she said, "Tell me." And Reymerig did.

"I can't stop crying for my daughter. I know all parents lose children, and we must never question God's Will, but I had no idea it would hurt so much. And the Indian attack! I don't mind losing the farm, but we thought the Wilden were our friends. We thought they were just like us only *nicer*.

"And now Hans wants to go back. I don't mind for myself, and I know that he'll need the boys, but I can't bear the thought of putting Marrichen in harm's way. She's only eight, and if I lost another daughter, I wouldn't want to live."

The women whispered through that night and many more. Anneke made inquiries, and at last they had a plan they were willing to share with Hans Jansen.

"Marrichen has never been as robust as the boys. It would be a shame if we took her all the way across the river to the farm and then had to bring her back again to see a doctor . . .

"Marrichen really can't help out on the farm as much as the boys can. She's almost in the way . . .

"I don't see how Marrichen will ever learn how to manage her own household out there in the wilderness. She'll never find a husband . . . "

"Why don't you let her stay here?" Anneke suggested.

"How could we do that?" Hans Jansen asked.

"Philip Gerritsen, who runs the City Tavern, is looking for a likely girl. He's a kindly man who won't work her too hard, and she would certainly learn a lot of good housekeeping skills there."

And so Marrichen, at age eight, was indentured to Philip Gerritsen for a period of three years. The contract was a fair one. She would begin work on New Year's Day, 1645—she would be almost nine by then—and in exchange for her services, Philip engaged to provide board, lodging, and clothing and also to have her taught sewing in such a manner as a father might do with his own child.

Anneke promised to look in on Marrichen at least once a week, and Marrichen knew she could always come and visit the parsonage if she were ever sad or lonely.

Anneke walked carefully across the frozen ground carrying yet another *pispot* of night soil out to the privy. She was alarmed to see a large man lying in wait in the early morning shadows at the foot of the orchard but relaxed when she recognized Manuel, whom she had not seen since the day of his mock execution. She was glad to see him but wondered why he hadn't come to the front door.

"I need to see the dominee, but I didn't think it would be a good idea for anyone to see me here today. The WIC slaves have an idea for a petition we want to submit to the council, but we need someone to help us write it."

"Come," Anneke said, "We'll go to the dominee."

Evert was also pleased to see Manuel. He asked after Michiel, the baby he had baptized almost two years ago, but he could see that Manuel had something else on his mind, so finally he asked, "What can I do to help you?"

Manuel hesitated, but at last he said, "You know the council has armed us slaves so we can help defend the colony against Indians."

"Firearms?"

"No, pikes and axes, but we think it is not right that men who have been enslaved should be required to defend those who are free. We wish to petition for our freedom."

Evert was aflame with enthusiasm. "It's brilliant!" he exclaimed. "We'll start with the Children of Israel being delivered from bondage in Egypt."

Manuel looked at him with concern.

"Evert," Anneke said. "That's not the way Manuel talks."

"Right," said Evert, sitting down at his desk and dipping a quill into the inkwell, "tell me exactly what you want to say."

"We don't want to say anything that sounds threatening, but we do want to make the point that we have all worked for the Company for eighteen–nineteen years now, and that all of us at one time or another have been promised our freedom. We all have families, and so long as we are enslaved, we cannot feed our children."

"Good points. I agree that you should make no threats, but I can make sure that the council understands that free men will defend their community more vigorously than will slaves. And who will be signing this petition?"

"All of us. All of the ones who were first brought here in 1627. There are eleven of us still living."

"Then let us write their names:

PAULO ANGOLA
BIG MANUEL
LITTLE MANUEL
MANUEL DE GERRIT DE REUS
SIMON CONGO
ANTHONY PORTUGUESE
GRACIA
PITER SANTOMEE
JAN FRANCISCO
LITTLE ANTHONY
JAN FORT ORANGE

and I will make a clean copy and bring it round tomorrow for all of you to make your marks."

Councilman Johannes la Montagne immediately grasped the seriousness of the situation. "Of course, we must grant them their freedom," he said. "They were never intended to be servants for life, and if we don't honor their request, we run the risk of their running off to join the Indians."

Kieft argued against the proposal, but at last the council settled on a compromise that even he could agree to. The official announcement would be made the following day, but Evert went to the slave house directly following the council meeting to share the details with Manuel and the others.

"Your petition is going to be granted . . . in part. You have to understand that you are Company property, and it is very difficult for Director Kieft to part with anything that belongs to the Company. Nevertheless, you and your wives are to be set free, and you are to be given plots of land so that you may support yourselves and feed your families."

"Where will those plots be?" Manuel asked.

"Out by the Fresh Water Pond to the north of the settlement."

"So . . . between the rest of you and the Indians?"

"Well, yes, and you must understand that you will be expected to pay for the use of the land: thirty schepels of maize and one fat hog per year. It is common practice in Europe for people who work the land to pay the landowner in kind. You will also be required, if needed, to come to the defense of the colony, but that is true for all colonists. You will be no different in that regard."

"In what regard will we be different?"

"The Company cannot quite bring itself to give you up altogether. You and your wives will be freed, but any children born to you will remain slaves."

A pounding on the door of the parsonage awakened them all in the middle of the night. Evert cautiously opened the upper half of the door, pistol in hand, but lowered his weapon when he saw that it was only Jochem.

"It's time," Jochem said breathlessly. "Tell Anneke to come quickly."

But Anneke, who had been expecting the summons, was already tying on her cap and apron. "Come, girls," she called to Katryn and Sytje. "Your sister's in labor."

Jochem lit their way through the moonless streets with a candle lantern. When they arrived, they found Tryn already in charge and labor well progressed. During the next hour, they rubbed Sara's back and held her hand while Tryn told her when to breathe and when to push, but Sara at seventeen was young and healthy, and soon enough Tryn announced, "It's a boy!"

Tryn cleaned the infant and swaddled him while Anneke wiped the sweat from her daughter's face and tidied her for bed. "Aren't you the proudest woman in the world?" she whispered.

When Tryn gave Sara her baby to suckle, the new mother exclaimed, "He looks just like his father."

Stroking her hair, Tryn said, "Don't worry. They all do at first, but he'll grow out of it."

The proud parents named their baby Hans. Someday he would be known as Hans Hansen or even Hans the Younger, but for now they called him Hansel.

Anneke sent Katryn to help her sister during her confinement, and during those crucial first two weeks of life she, too, stopped by daily, but the boy was robust, and soon they began making plans for his baptism.

"Who do you want for witnesses?" Anneke asked her daughter.

"Why, Oma Tryn and Aunt Marritje, of course," Sara answered.

"I was thinking of the men," Anneke said. "I think it would be a good idea to ask Evert and Director Kieft to stand up together. You know, let everyone see there's no animosity between church and state."

When Sara's lying-in period drew to a close and Hansel had been safely baptized, Anneke gathered friends and family together to welcome her grandson to the community. Marritje made her famous *kandeel* while Tryn made *koekjes*, and Anneke piled pillows behind her daughter's back and helped her into a clean new bed jacket. Katryn and Sytje tied gay ribbons onto Sara's bonnet, and Hans, clearly enjoying his ridiculous paternity cap, busied himself preparing a brandywine punch and setting out pipes for his gentlemen guests.

Hendrick the Baker arrived first with his wife Femmetje and their lively two-year-old Grietjen.

"My goodness, where *did* that child get her red curls?" Anneke asked as Femmetje handed her a basket of peach tartlets.

"She takes after my side of the family," Femmetje said, complacently patting her own graying locks.

A moment later, Dirck Holgertsen and Christine came. "Ma chère fille!" Christine exclaimed, giving Sara a big hug. "Just look at you," she said. "You were only a little girl when I first met you, and now here you are—a married woman with a baby of your own!"

Govert's wife Adriantje brought a silver saltcellar as a gift. She looked lovely as always in lavender silk with an elegant lace collar and a gold chatelaine at her waist, but she was pale and had dark circles under her eyes. She confessed she was recovering from a sick headache.

Annette Loockermans, dressed more simply in a skirt of vivid blue and a yellow blouse, gave the new parents a handsome brass candlesnuffer.

The women all admired the swaddled Hansel, lying in a cradle beside his mother's bed, and shared memories of their own travail. Adriantje told the horror story about how she had given birth to Maryken aboard the *Coninck Davit* during a hurricane. "Govert just loved the drama, but he said the next one had better be a boy. He was so disappointed when Janneken was born last year."

Anneke laughed. "Every man wants a son of his own. Don't worry. You'll have plenty of other chances."

"I hope so," Adriantje said. "You know we had to send my older son Hendrick to live with my sister Hester's family."

Anneke nodded. "We let our Jan go live with Marritje and Tymen because he wanted to become a carpenter."

"No, it wasn't like that. Govert was always so impatient with Hendrick, almost as though he were competing. He wants a boy, but he seems more tolerant of girls."

Femmetje arranged her tartlets on a pewter plate and began passing them around among the guests.

"Delicious," Annette complimented her. "You know, after three years here, I still can't get over how expensive things are. I suppose it's because everything has to be imported from Europe."

"Not everything," Femmetje said, putting the plate down on a small table. "The council sets the price of bread lower than it ought to be. What we really need is our own bakers' guild."

Hansel began to fuss, and Anneke picked him up and handed him to his waiting mother.

"You'll be needing a nurse now, won't you?" Adriantje said to Sara. "It's so difficult to find decent servants here. How do the rest of you manage?"

Anneke and Christine exchanged amused glances. "Well, mainly we just do everything ourselves," Christine explained, "but sometimes people hire the Angolan girls who live out by the Fresh Water Pond. They're always looking for work."

"Angolan!" Adriantje exclaimed. "Oh, I'd be afraid to do that! Dominee Michaelius warned us they are all thieving, lazy, and useless trash."

From time to time, clouds of pipe smoke and snippets of conversation wafted over from the men's side of the house.

Govert had purchased yet another farmstead.

Hans was explaining his plan to treat constipation with tobacco smoke using a contraption of his own design called the Kierstede Fumigation System.

"Sure hope you never have to use it on me," Hendrick the Baker quipped.

Christine walked over to Dirck and whispered, "I think Sara's getting tired. Can you make the last toast?"

"Right!" Dirck leapt to his feet and made sure that everyone had something to drink. Then he began, "The birth of a child is a sacred occasion not only for his family—his great-grandmother, his grandmother, and his parents—but for the entire community. May this child grow to be strong and healthy. May he be honest, loyal, and devout and live for all of his days in a world of harmony and peace. Welcome to the world, Hansel Kierstede."

In her role as *predikantsvrouw*, Anneke had been asked to do many strange things, but surely Evert's request that she pose to have her portrait painted must have been the strangest. Portraits, Evert told her, were all the rage in Europe, and now that they were expecting yet another child, he thought it was time they had their own made. Besides, he knew a young artisan from Leiden who was in need of work, so why not give it a try, heh?

At first, Anneke thought that the worst thing about having one's portrait painted would be sitting for hours unable to move. But no, the young man made a quick sketch while looking at her briefly through some sort of wooden box and then sent her on her way. No, the worst thing was that Evert wanted her to wear the dreaded ruff—ells and ells of linen bleached for hours and hours in the sun and then pinned into stiff pleats with scores and scores of pins. Marritje told her that ruffs were no longer fashionable in Europe and tried to talk her into wearing a simple collar, but in Evert's mind ladies of quality always wore ruffs. The regentesses of his orphanage had worn them, and so then would his wife. And he, of course, insisted on wearing his peruke, even though he knew that his fellow Calvinists despised wigs as a weak and effeminate affectation, which meant that she would have to clean and curl it and powder it all over again. She couldn't believe there was ever a time when she thought those nasty things were elegant.

The Eight Men narrowly approved Kieft's request to hire Englishman John Underhill to prosecute their war against the Indians.

"But wait," Wolfert Gerritsen had protested. "Isn't he the one who set fire to that Pequot village up at Mystic?"

"Exactly," Kieft said. "No one among us has comparable expertise in Indian warfare. We need to hire someone who knows what he's doing."

On a crisp October evening, one by one the Eight Men made their way through the nearly deserted streets to the parsonage. They met with Kieft every Saturday, but he routinely ignored their advice, and today they wanted to have a word in private. Evert was happy to put his home and his quill at their disposal, and they admired his florid style.

The Eight Men had sent two petitions to Amsterdam the previous year—one to the WIC and another to the States General—and Kieft was happy for them to be sent because Heaven knew he needed more resources. Conditions in the colony continued to deteriorate, however, and in desperation they wrote once again to the directors of the Amsterdam Chamber:

This is what we have, in the sorrow of our hearts, to complain of: that one man, who has been sent out, sworn and instructed by his Lords and masters, to whom he is responsible, should dispose here of our lives and properties at his will and pleasure, in a manner so arbitrary that a King dare not legally do the like. We shall terminate here, and commit the matter wholly to God, who, we pray and trust, will move your hearts and bless your deliberations, so that one of these two things may happen: that a Governor may be speedily sent with a beloved peace to us; or, that your Honors will be pleased to permit us to return, with wives and children, to our dear Fatherland.

"Well, that's clear enough," Jochim Kuyter said, "but I don't think we're going to be able to get Van Tienhoven to send it for us."

"Don't worry about that," Evert said. "I know a private merchant who will be departing soon. He is well disposed to me and will do us a favor."

And so Govert delivered the Remonstrance of the Eight Men to Amsterdam.

The portraits were finished. Everyone said they were wonderfully like, but Anneke, who had never seen herself in a proper mirror before and had no idea what she looked like, thought that her round red face looked like a baked apple topped with clotted cream and set atop an ornate piece of fine china—a homely dish on a fancy plate. Nevertheless, celebrate they must, so she and Evert invited Sara and Hans and Councilman Gysbert op Dyck to sup with them at the City Tavern. The evening started pleasantly enough. Anneke was pleased to see little Marrichen—now almost eleven—lugging a heavy pitcher of beer to their table. The child seemed well and when asked, said the work was not too taxing even though she missed her parents and brothers.

Soon enough, though, they heard the unmistakable English accents of John Underhill and George Baxter in the front room demanding service. Proprietor Philip Gerritsen placated the captain: "Friends, I have invited these persons with their wives; I therefore request that you betake yourselves to another room where you can be furnished with wine for money."

Underhill swore he would take his business elsewhere and left.

In the back room where Evert and Anneke were entertaining, table talk turned naturally enough to the English and their colonies to the north. A number of the English who had thought they wanted to live in a theocracy found it too rigid for their liking. That was why Anne Hutchinson, God rest her soul, had established her farmstead in Dutch territory where she would be permitted to worship as she pleased, but now she, too, had been massacred, a victim of the war.

"Did you hear how Captain John got himself excommunicated?" Evert asked. "He was in church, and he started eyeing a young woman. The Minister called him to account, and he almost got away with it by saying that he had not looked upon her with lust."

"And then?" Hans prompted.

"The Minister asked why he had not looked at the other women in similar fashion, and Underhill replied, 'Verily, they are not desirable women.'"

Laughter was still dying away when Underhill's braying was again heard out front. This time he had both Lieutenant Baxter and Thomas Willet with him, and he was not in the mood to tolerate any private party. He didn't care if there were women present. He wasn't interested in the dominee or the surgeon—they were boring toads—but Gysbert op Dyck was a fine fellow. Let him come out and fight if he dared.

Gysbert declined.

Underhill and his friends drew swords and started smashing crockery and hacking at the woodwork, forcing their way into the back room The landlady tried to hold them back with a leaded bludgeon, but it was useless, and soon they were in. Hans's instinct was to shield the women; Evert's was to thrust himself forward and fulminate.

Underhill yelled at Evert, "Clear out of here, Blowhardus, or I shall strike at random."

Willet bellowed, "Do you want to take Op Dyck's place? Come outside if you want to fight."

Evert threatened to call for the director, and Underhill, never at a loss for words, countered, "If the director comes here, 'tis well. I would rather speak to a wise man than to a fool."

Hans and Gysbert decided to call it a night.

Atrocities mounted. Captives were tortured to death in front of the church. More heads were mounted on pikes, and when one of them dropped, Christine's mother, Adrienne Cuvellier, viciously kicked it aside. Some of the spectators cheered, but many were appalled.

"Maman, that wasn't very ladylike," Christine chided.

"I'm impressed that an old girl like you can still kick so well," Marritje sniped.

Christine stopped speaking to her mother. Dirck asked whether she was worried about jeopardizing her inheritance, but Christine shrugged and said, "Just let her try it. I'll take them all to court."

Evert's sermons became repetitive, but there was an urgency about them that could not be denied: "Any man can create turmoil and set people one against the other, but to establish harmony again is in the power of God alone."

Kieft stopped attending church as did a number of his closest associates including Cornelis van Tienhoven and Olof van Cortlandt. He disrupted Evert's sermons by ordering the drummer to play during services and sometimes even wasted powder by firing the cannon.

Evert responded by refusing to take communion.

"Are you not worried that you might jeopardize your immortal soul?" Anneke asked.

"I am, but I'm even more worried that Kieft is jeopardizing the souls of all those who live in this colony. He and I have equal responsibilities. His are for governing the community, and mine are for its spiritual well-being. He has led half of our congregation into error, and I cannot receive communion until the rift is healed."

Captain John Underhill had no use for subtlety. He wanted the war to be over, and the surest way to end it was massive brutality. He led his men—Dutch and English—through the frozen wilderness until they reached a Wecquaesgeek settlement. When the moon was full, they attacked, but to his great annoyance, the Indians tried to defend themselves. *Oh well,* he thought, *might as well try what worked at* Mystic. His troops set the huts on fire and prevented any escape. Hundreds of people—men, women, and children—perished. As far as Underhill was concerned, his work was done.

Negotiations continued throughout the spring, and by August all of the tribes were ready for a cessation of hostilities. Treaties were made piecemeal, and then a general treaty guaranteeing a solid and durable peace was concluded. The usual gifts were exchanged, but Kieft's were not at all adequate to the occasion—either because he really was a mean and miserly man or because he simply couldn't afford anything nicer. Nonetheless, the war was over, and Director Kieft ordered a Day of Thanksgiving with church services to be held throughout the colony.

Now, Evert was always happy to have an occasion to preach an additional sermon, but under the circumstances, he really couldn't see that there was all that much to be thankful for. He began by reminding his congregants that the Wilden were not so called because they were "wild" in their hearts and manners and not because they lived in the wild like the beasts of the field, but because they had not yet had the opportunity to receive the Word of Jesus Christ. "Let us pray for mercy for all of the dead—both our own and those of the Wilden. I cannot name them all; I don't even know all of their names, but let us take Reymerig Volkerts who died on Long Island in one of the last skirmishes of the war as representative of them all."

The congregation gasped. Many of them had not yet heard of Reymerig's death.

The woman who wept because she wanted to believe the Wilden were her friends, the woman who loved her daughter so much that she had let her be bound over as a servant to protect her from harm now was dead . . . for no reason.

Many would be damned on Judgment Day because they killed innocent people.

Seven

PRINSES AMELIA

(1645–1648)

New Amsterdam

The war was over, but the conflict between the director and the dominee continued. Evert's eyes glistened as he approached the pulpit on Christmas Eve, but his step was firm and his speech steady. He had prepared a mild sermon, almost conciliatory, although he suspected that if Kieft attempted to disrupt the service, this might be one of those times when God chose to speak directly through him.

He mounted to the pulpit and began his oration . . . and the drumming started. Forgetting his prepared remarks, he thundered, "In *Africa,*" and then he dropped his voice almost to a whisper, "because of the excessive heat different animals *fornicate* whereby many *monsters* are generated." Raising his voice again, he continued, "But I know not in this temperate climate whence *these monsters of men* proceed!" Then, almost yelling, "They are the *mighty*, but they ought to be made *unmighty* who place their trust in the arm of the flesh and not in the Lord."

Half of the congregation was laughing or trying not to laugh while the other half sat gaping in horror. Anneke was mortified. She just wanted to get him out of there and home to safety. This was not going to end well.

Kieft spent the interval between Christmas and the turn of the year preparing a written indictment of every misstep Evert had ever made during the last twelve years. He ordered Evert to appear before the council in two weeks' time to answer the charges. Evert was beside himself.

"Listen, just listen!" he exclaimed. "He thinks he is *placed over me by God*. He is not placed *over* me. We are both employed by the WIC, but I answer *only* to the Classis in Amsterdam. No one in this colony is my *superior*."

He read the offensive missive to Anneke and then went back and read the worst bits over again. "He quotes a letter I wrote to Wouter in 1634. I thought Wouter was my friend. How dare he keep a personal letter I wrote to him as part of my official duties and hand it over to the incoming director with a warning about me?

"And here! Look here! He reproaches me with preaching while drunk."

Well, thought Anneke, *that is a tricky one*. Strictly speaking, Evert didn't drink any more than any other man, woman, or child in the colony, but it was true that it took him a drink or two these days to work up the nerve even to set foot in the fort. And it was undeniably true that with his florid turns of phrase and exaggerated flights of fancy he *sounded* drunk even when he was stone-cold sober.

"And what nonsense is this? He writes that at Adam Brouwer's wedding I spared not even my own wife or her sister."

Oh, Anneke remembered, *that was a particularly painful evening*. Evert was merry, as Kieft put it, and not having any salacious tales of his own to share, he dredged up the memory of Jacob Goyversen—the poor boy dead of yellow fever these many years—making Anneke a gift of cloth right after her husband died, and then he got an even bigger laugh by saying, "Well, at least you can't call Marritje a whore. She's never committed adultery for money . . . only for otters or beaver." If Tymen had still been alive, he would have killed him, and Anneke seriously wanted to.

There was never any question of Evert's appearing before the council, but this was a *written* challenge, and the following day he returned a *blistering* response, which Kieft dismissed as futile and absurd. Evert sent a second reply, which Kieft characterized as full of vain subterfuge, calumny, insult, and profanation of God's Holy Word.

Their feud, Anneke thought, might go on for a very long time.

Although everyone in the colony was aware of the hostility between the director and the dominee, some, like Adriantje Jans, had more important things to think about. Adriantje hated the New World. She found it coarse, dirty, and vulgar—not unlike her husband Govert, come to think of it. Fortunately, Govert was almost never at home, but on that evening he was, and Adriantje intended that they should have a serious conversation about their girls.

"What's wrong with them?" Govert asked. "They seem fine to me."

"We need to think about their futures," Adriantje explained, "to provide them with an education."

"How much education do they need? We have a schoolmeester here." Meester Adam had been deported some time ago for lewd behavior, but the new fellow seemed to be doing all right.

"All they can learn here is reading, writing, and catechism. There's no one to teach them singing, or dancing, or drawing. They're growing up like Wildinnen with no manners at all. They don't even know how to use a fork."

In Govert's experience *all* children between ages three and five were devoid of manners, but he could see Adriantje would not be placated, and she was, after all, the niece of the owner of the largest trading firm in Dutch America.

"We simply must take them back to Patria," Adriantje insisted. "Let my mother have charge of them. I'll stay with them just a little while until they are settled, and then I'll come right back here to you. That's what wives are for, after all."

Anneke was deeply concerned about the rift between the director and the dominee—worried about the outcome and worried also about the toll it was taking on her husband—but she, too, had no shortage of distractions. In February, they had celebrated Katryn's marriage to Willem de Kay, one of Govert's business partners. Anneke felt certain that Tryn, who had brokered the union but not lived to see it, would have been so proud.

Then, in late March, Anneke herself was brought to bed with a son, Pieter. By now, there was no point in pretending there was harmony between church and state, so they invited the leader of the opposition, Jochim Kuyter, to stand witness to the child's baptism along with family members Marritje, Sara, and Hans.

And then there was Marritje . . . When Tymen died falling from a quarterdeck last year, she had seemed inconsolable, but then yesterday she popped by the parsonage and brightly announced, "I'm pregnant."

Anneke looked up sharply from her churn and did some

quick calculations. She started to ask, "Do you know . . ." but caught herself in time and said simply, "Who?"

"Another carpenter, Dirck Cornelissen. We're going to publish banns next week."

"Well, that's all right then." Nobody much minded sex before marriage as long as the intentions were honorable.

"We're going to build on the property that Tymen patented last year"—Marritje, like Anneke, was land rich and penny poor—"and Dirck says he'll be happy to take over Jan's apprenticeship if you want him to."

Jan had enjoyed learning carpentry from Tymen, and Anneke was relieved that he would now be able to continue. She was also relieved to solve another little mystery she had never wanted to ask about. She had never understood how it was that Tymen and Marritje during the thirteen years of their life together had had but a single child, their daughter Elsie, born during the first year of their marriage. She knew some depraved women used artificial means to keep from having children so frequently, but Marritje clearly had not fallen into that perversion. She must just have been lucky.

It was difficult to go to the City Tavern in those days without running into WIC officials, so many of the disaffected took to congregating at the parsonage. Dirck Cornelissen helped Jan make a long trestle table and some benches that Anneke put out beyond the long rows of cabbage and onions amid the young apple and peach trees that she had planted, and in fine weather it was pleasant enough to sit there with a jug of beer and let off steam about the current state of the world without fear of nosy neighbors.

As the days began to grow longer in March, and the apple trees began to bloom, everyone was agog at the rumor that the WIC was finally going to recall Kieft and send the colony a new director.

"I hear the new guy's still Director of Curaçao," Jochem said. "How can he be in both places at the same time?"

"They must not think New Netherland's a full-time job," Hans said, refilling his pipe and lighting it again with a coal from the portable brazier where Anneke stood grilling sausages.

"Or maybe they couldn't find anyone else foolhardy enough to take it on," Anneke said, putting a fresh pitcher of beer and a platter with the sausages on the table.

"Well, so far they've given us an amiable drunk and a petty tyrant. So maybe if they gave us someone halfway competent . . ." Dirck Holgertsen said.

"Ha!" Dirck Cornelissen laughed. "They have no idea what we need. I hear the new one was a student of theology."

"Oh, great! That's all we need," Marritje said. "He and Evert can argue with each other in Latin."

"Did you all hear how the new guy lost his leg at Sint Maarten?" Jochem asked. "Blown right to bits, it was."

"That's not so unusual," Hans said, glancing at Jochem's leg. "Plenty of people lose legs, but I hear this fellow got himself an artificial one made—wooden with bands of silver."

"I wonder how he gets around," Christine said.

"I'm worried about how the Wilden are going to take to him," Anneke said. "They say they don't tolerate deformity of any kind."

The other main topic of interest that evening was the great white fish that had appeared in the North River about the same time the rumors of a new director appeared in the taverns.

"Have you seen it?" Dirck Cornelissen asked. "It's snow-white, but it has no fins, and it's absolutely huge."

"Seen it?" Dirck Holgertsen exclaimed. "I got close enough to watch it blow water out of the top of its head. What a stink!"

Evert said the Leviathan was a portent from God, but he hesitated to say what it portended.

The rumors turned out to be true. On a brilliant May morning four ships lay at anchor off the tip of Manhattan, and the grandest of them, the *Prinses Amelia*, carried the colony's new director. A crowd had turned out to gawk. Many were there to meet relatives or to take possession of trade goods, but for most the real reason for coming was to get a glimpse of Petrus Stuyvesant.

Dirck Cornelissen had eyes only for the *Prinses*. "Look at her, Jan!" he said to his nephew. "Isn't she the sweetest thing you've ever seen in your life? The others will all be sold or sent out again as privateers, but she's the one that's loaded with dye wood. She's the one that'll be taking our furs back to Amsterdam."

Jan was excited for a different reason. "I can't wait to see his wooden leg!" he exclaimed.

"I think it's a good thing he's bringing his wife," Marritje said. "A married man won't be so reckless with other people's lives."

"Is it true he married his nurse?" Christine asked.

"I heard he married some sort of relative," Marritje said.

"He married Judith Bayard," Anneke explained. "He went to stay with the family of his sister and her husband after his injury. The husband's spinster sister looked after him there, and now she's to be the first lady of New Netherland."

"I just want to get a look at his leg," Jan said.

At last the new director arrived, accompanied by his wife, Judith, already visibly pregnant. All eyes except Anneke's were on the famous leg. Everyone was expecting to see something grotesque, but he alit with practiced ease, glaring at anyone who attempted to assist.

While the others gaped at the artificial leg, Anneke studied the rest of the man. His clothing was plain, and his hair uncurled and unpowdered as befitted a Calvinist. His face was long and sallow, with a nose like a plowshare.

Kieft made an ill-advised attempt to save face by addressing the crowd as though they hated to see him go, but no one wanted to listen. They wanted to get the measure of the man who was to be their new master. At last, Heer Stuyvesant began to speak. He thanked Kieft for his service and made a solemn vow to the colonists that he would govern them as a father would his children.

"Sure hope he's not like my old man," Dirck Holgertsen muttered under his breath.

Evert made every effort to remain cheerful at home, but Anneke could tell he was confused and discouraged.

"I don't understand the man," he said, rocking Baby Pieter, who refused to be comforted. "His father was a minister. He studied theology at university, just as I did. I thought he would be sympathetic to my position, that we might be kindred spirits."

"How does he get along with Kieft?" Anneke asked, taking the squalling child from her husband and offering him her breast.

"He knows what Kieft has done, and yet he lets him sit at his elbow during council meetings. Kieft agrees with everything Stuyvesant proposes and lets it be understood that these are all things he would have done himself had he not been thwarted by malicious settlers."

"What kind of things?"

"Oh, you know, the usual. No alcohol to be served until

after services on Sundays, fines for knife fights, fence your garden, control your livestock."

"Surely that's all normal during a transition?" Anneke asked as she lay the sated Pieter in his cradle.

"It would be normal if Kieft hadn't committed acts of criminal treason. He ought to be arrested, but instead he wants to put the blame on his advisors. He's already requested permission to question the Eight Men in writing. And Stuyvesant maintains the oath of office sanctifies the position regardless of who holds it. Mynheer General, as he insists on being addressed, is charged with making and enforcing all rules and regulations both in civil and in ecclesiastical spheres."

"What does that mean for you?"

"On the bright side, it means he respects my office even though he may consider me a buffoon or even a traitor. But it also means he expects me to answer Kieft's charges before the council, and that I will not do. I answer only to the Classis in Amsterdam."

"What can you do?"

"The council has decided that the *Prinses* should be outfitted to return to Patria soonest. I can resign my position here and request passage on her. If I can make my case to the Classis, I will surely be vindicated."

"You wouldn't."

"I already have. Don't look so worried. It's not like the WIC ever paid me anyway."

Anneke pressed two fingers to the bridge of her nose and turned away shaking her head. *What were they supposed to live on then?*

Jochem wanted to have a private word with his brother Hans, so he invited him for a pint at Cregier's Tavern. They sat in a quiet corner away from the trictrac players.

"I'm worried about your father-in-law," Jochem said.

"Aren't we all? What's he done this time?"

"Nothing new, but Stuyvesant's out for blood."

"Because the Eight Men refuse to submit to Kieft's interrogation?"

"That and because Jochim Kuyter and Cornelis Melyn have requested permission to submit their own written questions to the members of the former council. I've seen the instructions that Stuyvesant has posed to his own advisors, and they leave no doubt about the outcome he expects: 'Was it ever heard or seen in any republic that vassals and subjects did, without authority from their superiors, conceive, draft, and submit to their magistrates self-devised interrogatives to have them examined thereon.' He means to see them hanged."

"Seems a bit harsh," Hans said. "What does this have to do with Evert?"

"He knows Evert wrote the Remonstrance of the Eight Men. He's charging Kuyter and Melyn with having copied it and then forging the signatures of the men who signed with their marks. He won't harm Evert here on Manhattan—out of respect for his position if nothing else—but once Evert sails on the *Prinses*, there's nothing to stop Old Silver Leg from sending instructions for him to be detained and tried in Patria. If that were to happen, it would cause no end of hardship for everyone he is connected with—especially Anneke."

"We've all tried to talk him out of going," Hans said. "I don't know what else we can do."

"I have legitimate business of my own in Patria. I plan to book passage on the *Prinses*, and then if he is molested in any way, I will at least be on hand to provide assistance."

Hans hesitated, but then he said, "Thank you, Brother. It is a kind and generous offer."

Anneke spent the evening before departure packing Evert's sea chest. He would need shirts and stockings, bed linen, and of course his silly peruke. Evert had written reams and reams of rebuttals to Kieft's accusations, but he wanted to pack them himself in an oilskin packet where they would be safe.

The following day, Evert wrote in large block letters that Anneke could read the name and address of his brother Cornelis in Leiden. "If anything happens to me," he said, "I want you to give him a Power of Attorney to collect my salary along with Roelof's and Tryn's."

Remembering her father who went to sea and never came home again, Anneke smiled broadly and said, "Don't be silly, what could possibly happen to you? You sailed to Africa and came back perfectly safe, and you will this time, too."

"You never can tell. Kieft might push me overboard."

They walked to the harbor arm in arm. A crowd had already gathered—some waiting to board, some seeing off loved ones. Jochim Kuyter and Cornelis Melyn had been convicted of lèse-majesté—offending those in high places—and imprisoned in the hold of the *Prinses*. Melyn was to be banished for seven years and fined three hundred guilders, and Kuyter for three years with a fine of one hundred and fifty.

Kieft was there with his entourage, still acting like he owned the place although he had to be worried about the investigations he would inevitably face back in Amsterdam. The WIC didn't take kindly to directors who squandered any of its resources—especially the human ones.

Hans and Sara were in the crowd with both of their boys. Three-year-old Hansel rode on his father's shoulders, and Sara carried Baby Roelof in a cloth sling. Hansel was excited that two of his favorite people—his Opa Evert and his Uncle Jochem—were both about to sail on this gorgeous ship.

Evert gave Anneke a quick kiss and offered a prayer for the safety of those who travel and those who remain. Then Jochem put his arm around her shoulder and whispered, "Don't worry. I won't let him come to any harm."

"Respect the post, not the person," Anneke murmured to herself as she looked around the crowded church. She knew Heer Stuyvesant regarded her as an ignorant Norwegian peasant and that he had invited her here today to witness the baptism of his son Balthazar Lazarus solely and exclusively to demonstrate to the community that there was no discord between state and church, Heaven forfend!

Except for Anneke, the other members of the baptismal party were almost all high-ranking WIC officials and council members: Lubbert Dinklagen, Johannes la Montagne, and, of course, the ubiquitous Cornelis van Tienhoven. It was laughable to think Anneke might ever take responsibility for the physical and spiritual well-being of small Balthazar. That lot would never let her get anywhere near him.

Still, it wasn't every day one got to see so many of the high and mighty gathered in one place. Govert, wearing a new suit of forest green with an elegant lace collar, arrived with his brother-in-law Olof van Cortlandt. Olof's wife Annette was still lying in, and Govert's wife Adriantje had elected to remain in Amsterdam, which, judging from some of the things Anneke had heard about that marriage, was probably just as well. Stuyvesant had established a new advisory board called with great originality the *Nine* Men. At least there was no mystery about how he came up with the number nine. He seemed to think there were three classes of people in New Amsterdam—merchants, burghers, and farmers—and he wanted three men to be appointed from each group. Govert had graciously agreed to represent the merchant class.

Elderly Jan Jansen Damen, trying to look like a youth again in his crimson waistcoat and shoes of white Spanish leather, entered with his stout wife Adrienne Cuvellier and her daughters Maria and Rachel. *How appropriate*, Anneke thought, *that Maria's husband Abraham Verplanck had gone bankrupt during the recent war that he had helped bring about.* Jan Jansen, of course, had been recruited for the Nine Men as representative of the burgher class. Some things just never change.

And then the star of the show, Balthazar, began to wail. *Oh, my!* thought Anneke, *such an unseemly breach of protocol. Whatever will the repercussions be?*

"Mamma, Mamma!"

Anneke looked up from her mending with a smile at the sound of Sara's voice. For half a moment she expected her daughter to burst through the door with some new and beautiful discovery, but one look at Sara's swollen face told her today's news was not going to be good.

"Mamma!" Sara flung herself to the floor and buried her face in Anneke's apron. "Have you heard?"

Anneke shook her head. She hadn't heard. She didn't want to hear.

"The *Prinses* has wrecked off the coast of Wales."

"Evert?"

"Drowned."

Anneke shut her eyes and put her hand over her mouth as though she might vomit. She lowered her head for a moment, but then she looked up again and asked, "And Kieft?"

"Him, too."

Anneke smiled bitterly. "Evert always did say that God had a sense of humor."

Eight

RETURN TO RENSSELAERSWYCK

(1648)

New Amsterdam

During the months that followed, Anneke had trouble sleeping. Every time she closed her eyes, she could feel cold black water closing over her head. Even waking, she saw Evert's comely features being dashed against the sharp rocks, and she tried to imagine what he must have experienced during those last moments. *Did he pray? Of course he did!* But not to bargain. Evert never bargained with God. No, he would have prayed for the souls of those about to perish. *Even Kieft's? Especially Kieft's.*

Kuyter and Melyn, Melyn and Kuyter. The two of them were among the twenty-one survivors while Evert and Kieft were among the eighty-six drowned. God's Will? Everyone seemed to think so. The wreck took place on September 27. How odd, how totally bizarre that even as she was promising to love and care for Petrus Stuyvesant's baby boy, her own husband was lying dead off the coast of Wales. Kuyter and Melyn made their way to Bristol and sent news of the tragedy both to the Old World and to the New. Their letter to the colony didn't arrive until January, and then it was copied over and over and passed around from household to household and read and reread to tatters, which upset Anneke a great deal because it made the preposterous claim that just before the end Kieft had sought out his two foes and said, "Friends! I have been unjust to you, can you forgive me?" Now Anneke had seen plenty of men meet violent ends before, and she knew for a fact that in the face of imminent death their *only* thought was not even how to save their souls but how to save their skins. Anyone who said differently was just a plain liar.

Of course, as far as Anneke was concerned, every death was violent. Tryn had died of old age in her own bed with Anneke and Marritje on either side of her, and it was still terrible to watch. She let Hans bleed her, which surprised her daughters because Tryn had always claimed bleeding did more harm than good, but then when Hans went to empty the basin, she whispered to them, "It'll go faster this way."

They sat with her, holding her hand and sometimes singing, until the light faded from her eyes, and then the awful rattle began. Anneke had heard the death rattle before—who hadn't?—but she had never understood it. Some people said it was demons fighting over the departing soul, but Anneke thought it was more likely to be the soul itself struggling to escape from the no-longer-needed body like a cicada fighting its way out of its useless first husk. They watched in horror as their mother's features—once so familiar and dear to them—began to twist and contort, all the while accompanied by the hideous rattle, until at last they found themselves encouraging her to hurry and finish her dread transformation. "You can do it, Mamma! Just let go, Mamma. You're almost there."

The other thing that upset Anneke was that even though eighty-six people had died, everyone spoke of the tragedy in terms of the fourteen thousand pounds of beaver pelts lost. Govert's partner, Seth Verbrugge, wrote to him from Amsterdam in November almost as soon as the survivors first brought news of the disaster. Seth's letter arrived in the colony only a few days after the earlier letter from Bristol, and Govert, to his credit, brought it around and read it to her. He apologized, saying, "You have to understand, Seth's a merchant," but Anneke actually found the account somewhat comforting. It seemed more factual than the first one—at least it didn't include any fanciful claims about Kieft's begging for forgiveness.

According to Verbrugge, the accident was the fault of a drunken first officer who mistook the Bristol Channel for the English Channel. *Maybe. That would be an awfully big mistake, but everyone agreed the weather had been foul, and the Bristol Channel was also known as the False Channel, so who could say?* After they went aground, they spent the night on that accursed ship while the crew made rafts to prepare for evacuation. *Rafts! Why didn't they spend the time actually evacuating instead of waiting for the incoming tide that broke the ship apart and killed them all?* But then it all came back to cargo. Verbrugge wrote that a few beaver pelts and corpses washed ashore, but the English seized them all. Anneke imagined wretched peasants, fishermen and their wives most likely, rushing back and forth to the shoreline like sanderlings to claim the bodies that rolled in with each successive wave and pick them clean. It was too much to bear.

Anneke was also troubled in those days by the general assumption that she needed to find another husband again as soon as possible. She had been married twice—once to the best man in the world, the love of her youth, and then to the most complicated man in the world, whom she had come to love dearly—but she saw no reason at this time of her life to chance matrimony a third time. Perhaps if Jochem had survived . . . But no, gentle Jochem had perished also, and Anneke, sinner that she was, hadn't even thought to ask about him when Sara first brought her news of the disaster. Jochem, she felt certain, would have married her, and it would have been a comfort to grow old with an affectionate friend, but that now never could be.

Anneke was genuinely touched when Petrus Stuyvesant stopped by the parsonage to offer his condolences. As she offered him seed cakes and fresh cider, she thought perhaps in the face of death they could at last talk about what a *good* man Evert really was.

And Stuyvesant made all the right noises. *Such a great loss . . . Pillar of the community . . . Thoughts and prayers . . . Anything Judith and I can do to help. . . .* But then he asked, almost in passing, "And how much longer do you plan to remain in this house?"

Anneke stared at her swollen knuckles and counted to ten before responding, "I see, Heer Stuyvesant, you come not to console the widow and the orphan but to evict them."

"Nothing of the sort," Stuyvesant spluttered. "I merely ask about your future plans. You may stay here as long as you like . . . within reason, but we have requested a new dominee, and when he arrives, this house will be allotted to him."

"A new dominee!" Anneke was outraged. "Couldn't you even wait until a decent period of mourning had passed? You must have submitted your request the instant you learned of my husband's death."

"No, mevrouw," Stuyvesant answered coldly. "I submitted my request the instant your husband resigned his position here. He was a contentious man. There was never any question of his returning to challenge civil authorities and foment dissatisfaction. I asked you politely what your future plans were, but since you spurn my civility, I will tell you outright that you must vacate. You may seek another husband, or you may move in with one of your married daughters, but you may no longer occupy this house."

"Can you count, mynheer? I have two unmarried daughters, a teenaged son who is but an apprentice, and four small boys. It is not in your power to force me to marry, and my married daughters, for all of their love of me, cannot take in eight additional mouths. Half of the people in this community believe you hounded my husband to death. If you drive us from our home, I will camp on your doorstep to show the world how you treat his wife and children."

"Now, now, there's no need for you to become agitated. Your mother's house stands empty. In view of your large family and difficult circumstances, I could offer it to you. What would you say to that?"

"My mother's house was scarcely large enough for a single woman. Seven fatherless children between the ages of three and seventeen, Heer Stuyvesant, all of them camped in front of your grand mansion crying out for justice."

"Your mother's house stands on a lot behind a larger house that is also empty."

"Grant it to me. Assign both houses and the land they occupy to me, and I will trouble you no more."

Marritje was impressed. "I can't believe you got the director of the WIC to give you two houses and a lot. That's going to make you an even more attractive catch. However did you do it?"

"Gentle feminine persuasion," Anneke explained. "That and a tiny hint of blackmail."

When Anneke finally felt certain of her plan, she invited Marritje, Sara, and Katryn with their children to join her for dinner. In a festive mood, she served herbed greens from her own garden along with capon stewed with prunes and root vegetables.

Marritje arrived first with fourteen-year-old Elsie and one-year-old Kees.

Sytje and Annetje swept Elsie away to a secluded corner of the orchard. They would take care of the smaller children while the adults ate, but for now they wanted to giggle and gossip.

Katryn marched into the front room as proud as a queen and deposited her infant Abigael in Anneke's lap. "Isn't she the tiniest, most perfect creature you've ever seen?" she asked the world at large.

And then Sara, apologizing for being late, joined them with six-year-old Hansel and year-old Roelfie. "Sytje, Annetje!" she yelled for her sisters. "Come take these boys away. I need to sit for a minute and talk with my mother in peace."

The food was delicious, the mood light, and everyone assured Katryn that Abigael was the most exceptional child they had ever seen. But then when the capon had been eaten and the cherry preserves cleared away, Marritje said, "So, Sister, what's the occasion? I'm pretty sure it's not your birthday. Is anyone getting married?"

"I've made a plan for my future," Anneke said, "and I want to share it with the three of you before the vanes of the gossip mill start spinning."

"Hooray!" Marritje cheered. "You *are* getting married. Who's the lucky fellow?"

Anneke shook her head.

"If she's not getting married," Katryn said, as she picked up Baby Abigael, "she must be getting ready to move into her new house, that's what."

"You're almost right," Anneke said. "I *am* getting ready to move . . . to Rensselaerswyck."

Anneke's announcement was met with silence. At last, Katryn said, "An unmarried woman can't just go off into the wilderness by herself, Mother. Think what people will say."

"I imagine there will be some disapproval, but yours are the only opinions I care about."

"Why would you do such a thing, Sister?" Marritje asked. "Surely it would be easier to marry."

"I'm forty-three years old. I am too set in my ways to put myself under the thumb of any man alive, and to tell you the truth . . . I no longer wish to have children."

"But why Rensselaerswyck?" Sara asked. "You have no friends or family there."

"Because I don't want to be pitied every time I step out the door. Because I don't want to live facing the fort and thinking about the men within who murdered my husband. Because I want to be able to go to church without feeling that Evert is about to step out of the pulpit and take me into his arms, and because I want to be able to worship my God without breathing the same air as Petrus Stuyvesant. Is that enough?"

"No, Sister, it isn't," Marritje said. "You have no means of support."

"I've thought it all through. I am responsible for managing both Roelof's Farm and Evert's, and I receive income from both. I intend to rent out my property here in New Amsterdam, and now that private parties are permitted to trade with the Wilden, I plan to give it a try."

"Oh, I remember, Mamma, from when we were little," Sara exclaimed. "You called it 'exchanging gifts.' You used to be so good at it!"

"But how can you do this to our sister?" Katryn protested. "Sytje will never find a husband up there in the wild. At least let her stay here with one of us."

Sytje slipped in from the side corridor, where she had just gotten Roelfie and Kees to go down for naps, and sat next to her sisters. "I've been listening from the back room," she said. "If this is what Mamma thinks best, I want to go with her."

"Let's get back to money," Marritje said. "Right now you don't have a stiver to your name."

"I've been in touch with Dominee Megapolensis in Rensselaerswyck. He has written to the Classis in Amsterdam to ask them to assist me. I'm the widow of a martyr. I have to believe they will come to my aid."

Aboard the Salamander

Anneke sat on her old, battered chest in the stern of the *Salamander* remembering her first journey up the North River. The mist-covered mountains looming in the distance were still spectacular, but the sense of awe she had once experienced was gone. She recognized her younger self, but when she thought about the things that young woman had done, it seemed like a story told about a different person.

The landscape hadn't changed all that much, but pretty much everything else had. For one thing, she was traveling with seven children who hadn't even existed eighteen years ago. Sytje, bless her, had accepted the decision to move with her usual good humor, and twelve-year-old Annetje was happy to follow her sister's example. Already seventeen, Sytje would need to be getting married soon, and Anneke shared

Katryn's fear that bridegrooms might be in short supply where they were going.

Fourteen-year-old Jan, to her surprise, had resisted the move the most. He told her he liked living with Aunt Marritje and Uncle Dirck. He liked working with Uncle Dirck, and he had friends now—*more like drinking buddies*, Anneke thought—and his mother had no right to uproot him.

Finally, Anneke sat the boy down and said, "Look, you really are the man of the house now. Carpenters are needed in Rensselaerswyck, and I need your earnings." And then, when he continued to grumble, she added, "How about this? I'll give you ten percent of everything you earn as pocket money?"

The little boys, Evert's sons, made no protest and were even excited to be going on such a long voyage. Willem, at nine, was a quiet child who preferred looking at books to going outside to play *kolf* with the other boys. Marritje had suggested he might be shortsighted, but since everyone knew spectacles were only ever worn by the elderly, Anneke rejected the notion. *Willem just liked holding things close to his nose, that's all.* Cornelis, at eight, looked the most like Evert with the same handsome features and plump red lips. Jonas, age five, was in constant motion, a whirlwind of curiosity, and three-year-old Pieter was just chubby and sweet. All of them different, and all of them loved.

The sloop was crowded today with other passengers as well—some of them traveling on business or to visit family and friends, some returning to their homes, and some, like Anneke, moving on. Anneke spotted her neighbor Hendrick the Baker and his wife Femmetje with Femmetje's older boy Piet and their own rambunctious redheaded daughter Grietjen and waved for them to join her.

Femmetje handed Grietjen off to Sytje and Annetje and then with a sigh of relief plumped herself down next to

Anneke. "I'm sorry for your loss," she began, but then she expressed her sympathy by relating how dreadfully she had suffered when her first husband died eight years ago.

Anneke knew Femmetje meant well, but she really wished she would hold her mouth. Trying to change the subject, she asked, "And what takes you and Hendrick to Rensselaerswyck?"

"Oh, you know, like everybody else, just trying to get ahead. A baker will never go hungry, but the prices are set so low in New Amsterdam right now and there are so many rules and regulations about what kinds of fancy goods you can make that it's hard to make a profit. If Rensselaerswyck were still just farms, we wouldn't risk it, but now that there's a community growing up around Fort Orange, we thought we'd give it a try. And there are so many more Wilden up north, and they'll buy anything that's sweet, and Hendrick's such a suyckerbacker, isn't he? But what about you? I don't mean to pry, but Evert must have left you pretty well off, heh?"

Anneke laughed. "The only thing Evert left me was a stack of books I don't know how to read and a pile of debts I can't pay."

Femmetje sat for a moment in embarrassed silence, but then she patted Anneke awkwardly on the knee and said, "Don't worry, dear. You'll never want for bread."

Anneke smiled her gratitude. It was the nicest thing anyone had said to her in a very long time.

On the second day of the voyage, Anneke noticed two young men, friends apparently, who were on their way home to Rensselaerswyck. One of them, Juriaen Westvael, was short and stocky with the muscular build and bronzed skin of a man who worked the land. The other, Pieter Hartgers, was taller with sandy brown hair that from time to time he brushed out of his eyes. All of the passengers enjoyed the men's easy banter and laughed at their jokes and quick wit.

"You fellows sound like you go way back together," Hendrick the Baker said.

"You might say that," Pieter replied. "We met back in Leidendorp."

"So did you come over together?" Anneke asked.

"Aw no, Juri beat me by a long shot," Pieter said. "He got here in '42, and I came two years later."

"But Pieter's done a lot better than I have," Juriaen said. "I'm still a hired hand, but he owns a brewery."

"That's only because I got a hefty loan from my brother Joost," Pieter said. "He's a bookseller back in Amsterdam."

"Joost Hartgers!" Anneke exclaimed. "My son-in-law has a standing order with him for pamphlets and books."

"The same," Pieter said, smiling. "I wanted adventure, and he wanted manuscripts, so he funded my trip, and I try to steer descriptions of the New World in his direction."

As travelers of all times have done, the passengers aboard the *Salamander* shared their provisions and told stories to pass the time.

"Who wants treats?" Hendrick shouted holding up a basket of pretzels.

"I do, I do!" The children all came running. They settled in a circle around him as he performed the familiar story of the little girl who tried to take some *koekjes* to her grandmother's house in the woods but got eaten by a wolf instead. He used the empty basket first as a cap for the grandmother and then as a disguise for the wolf and finally as a matchlock for the hunter who shot the wolf. When he finished, everyone—adults and children alike—applauded and told him what a wonderful performer he was.

"Let me take a turn," said Pieter Hartgers, pulling a small volume called *Moral Emblems* by Jacob Cats out of his travel bag. His audience sat entranced as he read them tales of "The Maid Who Soiled Her Dress" and "The Fish Who Imagined Himself a Whale." Anneke's favorite though was the verse that compared love to a game of tennis, and she fancied that Pieter was looking directly at Sytje when he read:

Mark, sweet maiden, when I strike,
And attend to what I say:
Tennis and Love's game alike
Need a quick return of play:
Who their pleasure most would know,
And in equal share partake,
In both games alike must show
Equal zest to give and take.

"That was just marvelous, Pieter," she said when he finished. "I would like so much to ask your advice about life in Rensselaerswyck. We will be staying at the home of Dominee Megapolensis until we have a place of our own. Might I persuade you to call upon us there?"

Heaven help me, she thought even as the words came out of her mouth. *I'm turning into my mother.*

Anneke did well to put her trust in Pieter Hartgers. Before they even reached Rensselaerswyck, he cautioned her about the new director, Brant van Slichtenhorst, who had taken control of the patroonship a few short months ago.

"He's older than you are," Pieter explained. "I'd say about sixty, and once he forms an opinion, he's absolutely unyielding, stubborn some would say."

"Sounds familiar," Anneke said.

"And right now I'd say that he's on a collision course with

Petrus Stuyvesant because he's formed the opinion that Fort Orange and the land it stands on are part of the Rensselaerswyck patroonship and therefore his to control. He's torn down a few of Stuyvesant's proclamations, and now he's started letting people build houses in the area directly in front of the fort."

Rensselaerswyck

When they docked at the Rensselaerswyck landing, Pieter helped Anneke and her children disembark and then hailed one of the carters who had come to greet the arriving vessel.

"Hoi, Tjerck," he said, handing the man a coin. "Can you take Widow Bogardus and her party to the home of Dominee Megapolensis?" And then he turned to Anneke and said, "You will need to get yourselves settled today, but if it's agreeable, I will call upon you tomorrow."

The following day, good as his word, Pieter sought out Anneke at the home of the dominee. They sat in the front room, next to the table with the Bible on it, looking out across the river at Fort Orange and the eight or so houses that now dotted the plain in front of it.

"You said you needed my advice," Pieter said. "How may I be of assistance?"

"I plan to settle here," Anneke replied, "and I want to go into trade."

Hiding his surprise, Pieter asked, "What do you mean by 'settle'?"

"I mean that I want to build a house and raise my children here. My son Jan is a trained carpenter. I hope you might help me find employment for him, but most of all I want your advice about trade. When I was much younger, I used to have friends among the Mohican, but I imagine that a great deal has changed since then."

"Trade is rough," Pieter said. "Our traders deal mostly with the Mohawk who bring their peltries here during the summer. The Dutch go into the woods to waylay the trappers, and sometimes they beat and kill them, and sometimes they are beaten and killed. It's no job for a woman."

"But there's no law against a woman trading."

"There's no law against women, but if you want any substantial profit, you will need to trade for alcohol or firearms, both of which are illegal."

"I don't want to get rich. I just want to provide for myself and my children."

By the end of the afternoon, they had reached a plan. Anneke would request housing on the plain in front of the fort where the two Indian paths met. She would not seek out male trappers, but she would build a structure behind her own house where the women who sometimes joined the trading parties might rest and ply their crafts. And if any peltries did come her way, rather than attempting to market them herself, she would consign them to Pieter.

"Thank you," she said when they parted. "This has been most helpful."

"It's an ambitious undertaking, and I admire your courage," Pieter said. "And now I have a favor to ask of you. Might I take your daughter Sytje walking this evening?"

"I don't know," Anneke said, laughing. "You'll have to ask Sytje."

Dominee Megapolensis accompanied Anneke to her meeting with Director Van Slichtenhorst the following day, but then he left her at the door, saying, "I think you will handle this best on your own."

When Anneke, dressed in her most somber church dress, entered the office, Van Slichtenhorst rose to greet her. "Ah,

Widow Bogardus," he said. "How nice that you are able to visit the dominee. A friend of your late husband, I believe. And to what do I owe the honor?"

Anneke took a moment to study the man in front of her. He was dressed plainly, as one would expect, with thinning gray hair pushed back from his balding forehead. His deep-set eyes stared fixedly at her face and figure. *Intractable*, Anneke thought, *but also impulsive, possibly even reckless.*

"Indeed, it is pleasant to see an old friend again," she replied, "but I have come for more than a visit. I plan to make my home here."

"With whom?"

"Hear me out, please. I may be a widow, but I am not a *poor* widow. I own property on Manhattan and on Long Island, but my affection remains with Rensselaerswyck, where I first settled eighteen years ago at the request of the late Heer Van Rensselaer. I admire your dedication to protecting the interests of the patroonship, and I know how difficult it has been to attract settlers to this remote location. I bring with me seven children including daughters of marriageable age and a son who is a carpenter. Grant me a lot where I might build, and I will improve the land and pay rent just like any other settler and help you make this land to bloom."

"Perhaps on the south side of the fort . . ."

"No, mynheer, on the north side at the junction of the two Indian paths."

Anneke brought Pieter with her to meet the surveyor who lay out the boundaries of her new lot. The land about was hilly and covered by tall trees, but the area adjacent to the path was fairly flat—a good place to build. Together the two men paced off an area roughly three rods long and six rods in length.

"Good," Anneke said. "There'll be enough room for a house, a garden, and a bleaching field."

"It's a good location," Pieter agreed. "I've requested the lot directly opposite yours."

After the land had been surveyed, again following Pieter's advice, Anneke hired the English carpenter Clabbord to build her new house.

"What barbaric names the English have," she exclaimed to Pieter. "Why would anyone name a child Clabbord?"

"Ha," Pieter laughed. "His real name is Thom, Thomas Chambers. Clapboard's a kind of siding the English use on houses. Thom was the first one to start using it here, and now that's what everyone calls him."

Anneke insisted that Jan come with her to meet Clabbord at the future building site. "I want the house here," Anneke said, pointing to a scrubby area between two sapling walnut trees. "We need both a cellar and an attic, but for now we'll start with just two rooms and everything can be wooden until bricks become available. Later on, I'll want to add a side aisle and some outbuildings."

"Can do," Clabbord said laconically. "Twelve beaver."

"Six," Anneke countered, putting her hand on Jan's shoulder and pushing him forward. "Six beaver and six months of work from a skilled assistant."

"But, Mam," Jan whined after Clabbord had left and they were alone again. "You promised me ten percent of my earnings."

"You'll be receiving that and more," Anneke said. "It's called room and board."

Nine

ACTS OF GOD

(1648–1652)

New Amsterdam

Govert was furious. It wasn't fair that he should have to support a wife—a very expensive wife—in Amsterdam and pay for sex here in the colony. He took a Wildinne by force once and enjoyed it, but one couldn't go around doing that sort of thing all the time. *Perhaps he should purchase an Angolan?*

That little weevil Seth Verbrugge had the nerve to write to Govert as though he were a puppet master: "We all, your devoted shipowners, want to ask you to please keep Heer Stuyvesant as a friend and ensure always to stay in his good graces even if we are the topic of talks." All right, he had done as they asked. He dined with Stuyvesant almost daily, and now he wanted his wife back. But no, then he got another letter from Seth saying his request had upset Adriantje, and with her sick headaches she could not possibly be expected to make another overseas crossing. *Headaches! If it weren't for her headaches, they'd have a dozen children by now, and all of them boys*. And *then*—the biggest insult of all—Seth offered to send Govert camphor *to quell the rising of the flesh.*

The Verbrugge clan was just full of surprises. Govert was reading a *lengthy* business letter signed by Gillis and son, which probably meant Seth had written it. They responded to Govert's request for trade goods—kettles, axes, and market wares—saying, "We can't do that."

They had told Govert to ingratiate himself with Heer Stuyvesant, but then they expressed horror and outrage when they learned the Heer now was indebted to them for twelve thousand guilders. What if he were recalled? What if he died? He would never repay them then, and they would lose so much money.

And this was the part Govert found the most infuriating: "From private letters you surely will have learned with sorrow about the death of your wife." *Well, as a matter of fact, he* had *already received the news—apparently she was serious about those headaches—but what if he hadn't?* And then, after practically forbidding him to return to Patria to collect her when she was still alive, they now assumed he would want to return to put his affairs in order and gave him elaborate instructions for calling in debts and divesting himself of trade goods. They didn't say it in so many words, but it was clear to Govert that now that he was no longer a member of the family, they wanted to recall him to account for himself, and that he would not do.

What to do, what to do?

For once, Govert was actually enjoying writing to Seth Verbrugge:

"It seems that the friends are disgruntled with my service . . .

"It is well known to the friends that I had to leave my sweet and beloved wife . . .

"The friends have given me the freedom to come back home, for which kind favor I cannot thank the friends enough. I would have come, but as it pleases the good God, who reigns over all, I have been given a new partner. Therefore, friends, please excuse me."

And put that in your pipe, dear friends, and suck on it!

Rensselaerswyck

Anneke's new house in Rensselaerswyck was thatched and ready just in time for her to host Sytje and Pieter's wedding celebration. The wedding party was still nursing hangovers when Sytje received a letter from Sara. Aunt Marritje's husband Dirck, Sara wrote, had swung an axe into his leg and despite Hans's best efforts the wound had putrefied. Hans had offered to amputate, but Dirck had refused, saying if he must die, he would just as soon do it with both legs attached.

"Oh, Mamma," Sytje said when she finished reading. "You must go back to New Amsterdam. Aunt Marritje needs you so much!" And so they agreed. Sytje would take care of the younger children while Anneke was away in the south comforting her grieving sister.

New Amsterdam

Anneke hired a cart to take her from the river landing to Sara's new house on the strand. As they drove past the rundown fort and turned onto the strand where the gallows once stood, she thought yet again about how much everything had changed even during the short year she had been away. Many of the old wooden houses were now faced with yellow brick, and their thatched roofs replaced by tiles. There was a new cattle market now alongside the fort, and everywhere she looked—people, people, people.

Traveling slowly up the strand, Anneke spied Sara sweeping the stoop of her step-gabled house. She called out, and Sara, dropping her broom, ran to her mother, helping her from the cart and taking her heavy travel bag.

"Mamma!" she exclaimed. "Why didn't you tell us you were coming? How long can you stay? Come see the house. Come see your grandsons. How's Sytje? Is she in a family way? I think I might be."

"Stop," said Anneke, laughing. "One thing at a time. Everyone's fine. They all send their love. Now give me a glass of beer before I drop of exhaustion, and then show me this new house I've heard so much about. This corner facing the East River is a perfect location!"

"Isn't it just? It's so much easier for Hans to receive his patients here, and it's so convenient for traders coming from Breuckelen that the burgher council wants to build a regular market right in front of our house."

"That'll be nice for you," Anneke said. "You always did enjoy chatting with the Wilden."

"I still do," Sara said, "and Hans is going to build a wildenhuysje at the back of the garden plot so on market days there'll be a place for the women to sit and work. But what am I going on about? Let's get you inside and give you something to drink."

When they entered the house, they found Hans preparing to shave a crew member of one of the outbound merchant ships. As he honed the razor, his seven-year-old assistant Hansel ran to fetch warm water and towels while his younger brother Roelfie rolled marbles across the terra-cotta flooring.

"Mother!" Hans greeted his mother-in-law. "What a pleasant surprise. Just let me finish up here—I still need to draw a couple of teeth and stanch the blood—and then I'll join you for dinner."

As the women passed through the front room, Anneke had time to notice the Delft tiles surrounding the hearth and a hand-tinted map of the New World hanging on the dark-green wall. Continuing out through the back room, they passed into the garden, and here Anneke was surprised to see not only the familiar rows of cabbages and parsnips but also a rectangular bed with trees and shrubs and smaller plants she didn't recognize. "What are you raising?" she asked.

"It's called hortus medicus, a medicinal garden," Sara explained. "Many of the simples that Hans imports from Europe can be grown here, and there are other beneficial plants that are found only here. We didn't want to plant anything at the WIC rental, but now that we have a place of our own, I plan to take over the apothecary side of the family business. Tell me what ails you, and if Hans can't cut it off, I can at least make a salve to make it feel better."

Dinner that afternoon passed in a chatter of shared news. "He's building a wall, Stuyvesant is, across the tip of the island," Hans said. "I suppose it might deter a few Wilden," he said, shaking his head, "but I don't see how it's supposed to protect us from the English."

"But tell us, Mamma, about Rensselaerswyck," Sara said, ladling a portion of stewed pigeon onto her mother's plate. "What's it like there, and how is Sytje? How do you manage?"

"You know, it's a funny place, but it suits me," Anneke said. Then she laughed. "If you look from a hilltop at the way the roads come together, it looks like a fyke net."

"You mean an eel trap?" asked Hans, who was a city boy.

"Exactly," Anneke said. "Imagine a funnel right by my house. The settlers swim in through the funnel, and then they don't know how to get out again, except most of them don't really want to. The people there are somehow lighter, less serious than they are here. They have funny names for everything. They call your sister's house Het Huysmusgen, Little House Sparrow, which suits her so well, and they call mine De Gierswerelt, Vulture World."

"How rude!" Sara was shocked.

"I don't mind. I think it's because I go to so many estate sales to buy trade goods, either that or because I've gotten so stoop-shouldered with age, but if people tease me, it must be because they like me."

"So you're really trading?" Hans asked, moving a tray of candied walnuts out of the reach of young Roelfie.

"On a small scale. As long as I'm not greedy, I think I'll do all right. I buy things that no one else wants like broken copper kettles, and then Indian women take them from me for the metal. But tell me this," she said, "all of this time we've been talking no one has said a word about my sister. Has something awful happened to Marritje? Is she terribly devastated?"

"Nooo . . ." Sara said slowly. "I think Aunt Marritje's fine. She tells us she means to remarry."

"So soon?" Anneke was surprised. "Don't tell me she's pregnant again."

"I don't think so."

"Then why the haste and who's the man?"

"Govert Loockermans."

Anneke marched up the strand to Marritje's house so fast she got a stitch in her side. In a better mood she would have enjoyed the morning light sparkling on the East River, the tiny green leaves beginning to appear on the peach trees, and the fat red-breasted thrush searching for worms in the underbrush, but this day she was indifferent to the beauties of God's world. She was on a mission to save her sister.

When she reached Marritje's house, the top half of the door stood open, so she reached in to unlatch the bottom half and let herself in.

"Are you crazy?" she yelled from the doorway.

Marritje emerged from the scullery drying her hands on a piece of sacking. "I'm glad to see you, too," she said.

"He's only marrying you for your property."

"Are you speaking of my betrothed? Govert has plenty of property of his own."

"The man's a smuggler and a thief. He sells firearms to the Indians. He's a murderer."

"Well, maybe I'll be a good influence on him."

"Marritje, this is no time to be flippant!"

"And this is no time for you to interfere in my affairs. Listen, Anneke, Govert Loockermans is one of the richest men in the colony. When I am his wife, I will have a grand house and gowns of silk and all the servants I could possibly want. I will dine off fine porcelain at the right elbow of Petrus Stuyvesant, and my daughter Elsie will marry any man she chooses."

"So you would ruin yourself just for money."

"I'm not ruining myself. I actually like Govert. We have fun together, and he needs me. He has two motherless daughters in Amsterdam. When we're married, he plans to fetch them, and then we're going to build the grandest mansion imaginable, fit for a pirate, right here on the strand. Don't judge me, Sister. I'm not doing anything you haven't done, just doing the best I can to get by."

Anneke let herself be persuaded to stay for the wedding and, at Marritje's insistence, stand witness for her sister as her closest relative. She had to admit that Marritje looked downright regal in her gown of brocaded satin damask with its long, ruffled sleeves and high-standing lace collar. And Govert, dressed entirely in luxurious black except for his crimson cravat, looked like a veritable pillar of the community. Following the ceremony, Anneke stood—she hoped for the last time—in the church inside the fort and greeted Petrus Stuyvesant and other high-ranking guests with all the civility she could manage. And when Govert kissed her on the cheek and called her his dearest sister, she even managed not to gag.

Rensselaerswyck

Willem started coughing and said he didn't feel well enough to go to school, so naturally Cornelis wanted to stay home as well. Anneke suspected Cornelis of malingering, but his forehead did feel a little warm, so in the end she agreed. She wasn't worried, though, until Annetje came in from the milking, frightfully pale, and said she hadn't the strength to carry the bucket.

"Let me see your tongue," Anneke said and blanched when she saw the telltale spots. Looking out the window, she saw Sytje bringing the little boys, Jonas and Pieter, home from mushroom foraging.

"Stay away," she shouted from the window, "kinderpockjens. Keep the boys. Don't let them get near us. Jan's working down by the first kill today. Find him and tell him to stay with friends."

"But Mamma," Sytje protested. "You'll need help."

"God has spared me once before," Anneke said, throwing back her head and pointing to the line of pockmarks along her jaw, "and He will this time as well, but I'll need you to bring us food. Leave it on the doorstep, but don't come in, and I will put a white kerchief in the window every morning so you know we're still alive."

She turned and closed both doors and all of her shutters to keep the noxious airs out. Annetje already had a high fever and was verging on delirium. Anneke gave her willow bark tea and made a vinegar compress to put on her forehead.

"Your sister's very sick," she said to Willem and Cornelis, "and you're probably going to be also. I'm going to make a bed for you to lie on, and I want you to listen to me carefully and do exactly as I say."

During the next three weeks, Anneke lived in a sort of twilight, sleeping at odd intervals, and only knowing that day had come when she heard Sytje leave food on the stoop. She spooned broth into her children's mouths and bathed their swollen faces with vinegar. She made soft mittens to keep them from scratching themselves and put pumpkin poultices on their sores, once even tying Willem's hands to the bed to make him lie still.

And on the day she saw the blood starting to seep from Annetje's eyes and gums, she fell to her knees and begged God to spare her youngest daughter, but God, as usual, was implacable. She beat her head against the wall and tore her hair, crying, "Why am I so cursed that I cannot keep even one small girl safe from harm?" But then she heard Cornelis cry out for her, and she knew there was no time for her to spare on tears.

She wrapped Annetje's frail body in a strip of white linen, cut off a lock of her golden hair to put with other keepsakes in her *notas*, and put a black kerchief in the window as a sign to Sytje. By evening the boys' fevers had broken, and the following day she could see their pustules beginning to recede. The crisis had passed, and both boys would live. Willem would be lightly marked, but her beautiful Cornelis was scarred for life.

The settlement was devastated by the smallpox epidemic. Some households, like Sytje's, had been spared, but most had lost family members, sometimes a parent, but most often children. Anneke had no way of knowing, but she had a feeling the Wilden had suffered as much if not more than the Europeans. Fewer Indians came to trade, and women who used to bring two or three children with them now came alone. One woman, whom Anneke recognized from previous visits, pointed at Cornelis's ruined face and then looked around the yard as though searching with her eyes for Annetje. When she couldn't find her, she covered her face with her hand and lowered her head in what Anneke took to be a gesture of sorrow. Anneke sent her away with a small pot of raspberry preserves. She wasn't trading, no. It was a gesture made from the heart, and she expected nothing in return.

When the ice on the North River broke the next spring following the epidemic, Marritje made the trip north to visit her sister. Sytje met her at the landing and brought her up to Anneke's house at the junction.

"Just like old times," Marritje said, walking through the front of the house to the scullery where Anneke was bent over a churn.

"Just like," Anneke said. "Older but no wiser. Come take your cloak off. I suppose you'll be wanting some tea."

"No tea, but some buttermilk would be nice. I'm sorry you lost Annetje."

Anneke nodded and turned her head away, trying to fight back a tear. Sytje put her arm around her mother's shoulder and hugged.

"And I'm sorry Sara lost Baby Anna," Marritje continued.

"All parents lose children," Anneke said gruffly. "Tell us some good news."

"My Elsie's engaged to be married. He's a good man, a merchant. I think they'll be happy together. And Anneke, your Katryn has put off mourning and found herself a new husband: Lucas Rodenburg."

"Rodenburg? You mean the Vice Director of Curaçao?" Anneke asked.

"None other," Marritje confirmed. "Second only to Heer Stuyvesant himself."

"Oh, Mamma!" Sytje exclaimed. "Just think: our Katryn—the first lady of Curaçao with all the sugar she can eat! Mamma, why do you look so serious? Say something."

"I'm very happy for Katryn," Anneke said, "of course, I am," but she kept thinking to herself: *there's another daughter I'll never see again.*

"But tell us about yourself, Auntie," Sytje said. "How's your grand house coming along?"

"Oh, it's wonderful . . . but . . ." Marritje unexpectedly got a catch in her voice.

"Oh, Sister! Don't cry!" Anneke was horrified. She had never seen Marritje even slightly downcast before—not even at funerals.

"It's just that I don't feel like it's my house anymore. Govert and I used to have so much fun when we were living in the old house that Dirck built—just the two of us with Elsie and Baby Kees. And we had a wonderful time designing the new house. It was almost like a competition to see who could come up with the most outlandish ideas. There are two wings—one for each of us—and we've built a brick stove right next to the hearth and moved the bake oven from the outdoor kitchen to the inside of the house. Govert actually wanted to hang gilt-leather coverings on all of the walls, but

I said, 'Absolutely not! There'll be insects nesting in them within a week!' Tiles are so much prettier and easier to clean!"

"It sounds like a fabulous house, Sister. Why are you sad?"

"Govert didn't want to fetch his girls until after his contract with the Verbrugge Firm expired. Didn't want to be at the firm's beck and call, he said. And he said some other strange things about reclaiming his property and the girls needing to be acclimated before putting them on the marriage market, but I thought he was teasing, so I kept telling him to hurry up and bring them home."

"And he did . . ."

"He did. And not only the girls but also the grandmother who raised them. And to hear her tell it, her daughter was an absolute saint, and Govert is responsible for her death."

"Oh, dear . . ."

"And I'm an interloper. Lysbet Setten thinks she's the mistress of the house, and she treats me like a maidservant."

"I'm sorry, Sister. How's Govert handling it?"

"By staying away as much as possible."

"But the girls are sweet . . ."

"I suppose they are. But they've been raised in such a strange way that I scarcely recognize them. They won't drink beer—makes them gassy, don't you know. No, they have to have tea served in porcelain cups with sugar comfits on the side. Dining midmorning is old-fashioned. They want to dine midafternoon, and each girl must have her own plate and eat with her own fork. And you simply wouldn't believe all of the fancy dinnerware that Lysbet Setten has brought with her! Ordinary roemers aren't good enough for her. No, she prefers Venetian goblets, and she even has a couple of gilt goblet holders that she sets full glasses of wine on. Looks like an accident waiting to happen!"

"But you still love the house, don't you?" Sytje asked.

"I used to, but now I don't even recognize it anymore. Lysbet's covered all of the walls with oil paintings. Govert used to order a few pictures every now and then. He'd always say, 'Ships or seascapes, whatever you think is best,' but *she* puts up dead fish and vegetables, and all they do is remind me that I need to go back out to the kitchen and fix dinner."

"I'm sorry, Sister," said Anneke, trying to suppress a very unchristian surge of smug satisfaction. "Why don't you stay here with us over the summer? Maybe by fall things will be better."

"I'd love to, but I'd be afraid Lysbet might change the locks. Besides, this is a bad time for me to be away. I have to get ready for Elsie's wedding, and . . ." She put her hand on her abdomen. "I really don't want to lose this one. Govert's waited so long for a son."

Ten

BEVERWYCK

(1652–1658)

Rensselaerswyck

For the nearly four years Anneke had been living in Rensselaerswyck, she had made a point of having as little as possible to do with Director Brant van Slichtenhorst. True, he had done her a favor by permitting her to build at the junction, but he impressed her as arrogant and unpredictable, like every other director she'd ever met, and she preferred to keep her distance. That didn't keep her from hearing details of the director's ongoing feud with Petrus Stuyvesant from Pieter, whose civic duties kept him in the thick of things, and it didn't keep her from drawing obvious conclusions on that New Year's Eve when celebrating soldiers at Fort Orange shot burning arrows into the thatched roof of Van Slichtenhorst's house.

"That's awfully bold," she said to Pieter after the fire had been put out and the excitement died down.

"Things can't go on like this," he agreed. "Something's got to change."

And change they did. Within a few short months Stuyvesant arrested Van Slichtenhorst and claimed the illicit settlement surrounding Fort Orange in the name of the WIC. He ordered all of the dwellings closest to the fort demolished and set the WIC soldiers and the villagers to building a stockade around the occupied area. Henceforth, he proclaimed, the newest Company town would be known as Beverwyck.

"Beverwyck!" Anneke lamented when Pieter came home with the news. "I moved here to get away from the WIC. Is there no place to run?"

"You could push on to Hartford," Sytje said, burping her colicky infant, Rachel, "but you'd have to learn English."

"Don't tease," Anneke said. "This will affect all of us, you and your daughters included."

"I think maybe it won't be so bad," Pieter said thoughtfully. "Stuyvesant has just acquired a valuable asset, and he will want as little disruption as possible. I understand he plans to give those of us who are already established here patents to the land we now occupy."

"Come now, Pieter," Anneke said. "You know he's not going to give a widow woman patent to anything."

"I sit on the burgher council," Pieter said, "and if I guarantee to pay four beavers a year in taxes for you, I don't see why anyone would care whose name the patent's in."

On the second Sunday in April, Anneke put on her dark-gray church dress and fastened her book of Psalms onto her belt. She let Willem carry her foot warmer and handed her folding stool to Cornelis. Then, with Jonas and Pieter trailing behind, they all set off for church.

When they reached the patroon's house, they climbed the outer staircase to the storeroom where people would gather to worship until such time as a proper church could be built.

Anneke greeted some of her neighbors and then opened her stool and settled herself comfortably as far from the pulpit as courtesy permitted. *How nice*, she thought, *to be able to doze through the dominee's sermon like a normal person and not have to anxiously monitor every word that comes out of his mouth.*

On that particular Sunday, following the usual service, Pieter's friend Juriaen Westvael and Marrichen Hanss, a newcomer to the community who had been working for Jacob the Brewer for the last six months, joined their hands in marriage. The bride looked familiar to Anneke, but all young women looked alike anymore, so she didn't give it much thought.

Ordinarily, the party that followed the wedding would have been held at the home of the bride, but since Marrichen's father lived on far-away Long Island, Pieter and Sytje invited everyone to come to their place instead. Long trestle tables had been set out in the orchard behind their house with vats of sour cabbage, glistening links of sausage, great wheels of cheese, and barrels of beer. A new neighbor, Sander Glen, brought his small pipes and treated them all to raucous dance music.

Anneke sat down on a bench beside Sytje, who was shoveling porridge into Baby Rachel's drooling mouth while Rachel's big sister Jannetje lay on the ground pretending to be a crying baby in a bid for their mother's attention. "Here, Jannetje, come to Oma," Anneke said, and took her three-year-old granddaughter onto her lap. "I was just wishing I had a big girl to help me eat this cruller. Do you want a bite?"

A moment later, the bride, already flushed from drink and dance, came over to sit with them. "Do you not remember me, Mother Bogardus?" she asked.

"You seem familiar," Anneke said. "Perhaps you could refresh my memory."

"My family stayed with yours during the Indian unrest. You were very kind to us."

"Now I remember," Anneke exclaimed. "You're the little girl who worked at the City Tavern. Imagine that! Whatever brings you to Beverwyck?"

"Pappa's new wife didn't care for me, so Pappa thought it would be best to send me here to work in Cousin Jacob's brewery. It's all right," she said, responding to Anneke's look of concern. "I know more about tapping than I do about farming, and anyhow . . . that's how I met my Juri."

"We're so glad you're here," Anneke said, warmly pressing Marrichen's hand. "How lovely to have you as a neighbor."

"Except we won't be here long."

"How's that?"

"Well, your husband," she said, nodding at Sytje, "has taken over Juriaen's lease on Papscanee Island, and next week we plan to join the group that's heading south to settle on the Esopus Creek. Juri is going to manage a farm there for the Heer General."

"But how is that possible?" Anneke asked. "The Esopus is where the River Indians farm."

"Oh, I know! Isn't it marvelous? The land has already been cleared, and now all we have to do is pop our crops into the ground and watch them grow."

On the far side of the orchard, a group of men clustered around Thom Chambers. Young Jan, who had already worked on several projects with the English carpenter, was proud of their association and, already a bit in his cups, made a point of showing how close they were by addressing the older man as "Clabbord" as often as possible.

All of the men were disquieted by Chambers's decision to move so far south of Fort Orange to the area they called the Esopus.

"I wouldn't think anyone would want to live so far away

from the fort," Hendrick the Baker said. "Aren't you afraid of the Wilden?"

"Not a bit of it!" Chambers said. "They signed a document assigning the land to me, so it's all fair and square. And besides, Kit Davis will be coming with us, and he spends more time with the Wilden than he does with the Christians."

"But this is where the Wilden come to trade," Jacob the Brewer said. "How can you support yourself so far from civilization?"

"This is where the Wilden come to trade when they're not busy fighting each other and when there are beaver to be had, but do you remember how bad things were last year when all the beaver disappeared? I made the case to the burgher council in New Amsterdam that when the Wilden go away, there will be more money to be made in wheat and tobacco, and they agreed to let me try."

"But it'll take forever to get there," Tjerck the Carter said. "How long will it take to haul everything you own over those Indian trails?"

"I don't mean to haul anything, simpleton. I've hired barges to do the hauling."

"But tell 'em the truth, Clabbord," Jan blurted out. "Tell 'em what you really mean to do there."

Thom grinned at his young protégé. "Why, I mean to become lord of my own manor, Johnny Boy, lord of the whole stinking manor."

Ne'er-do-well Jan had never lacked for work in Beverwyck although for a time he seemed bent on drinking all of his earnings. Then, just about the time he turned twenty, he took himself in hand and put aside his boisterous ways. He undoubtedly benefitted from the example of his brother-in-law Pieter, who first helped him patent a parcel of land in his own name and then recommended him to the magistrates as town surveyor responsible for laying out boundaries and borders for others. And after two years of respectable work, he was able to come home to his mother with extraordinary news.

"Mamma," he said, kissing Anneke on the cheek. "I've asked Pieter and Sytje to come over this evening. Pieter and I have something to tell you all."

After the *hutspot* had been eaten, pewter dishes scoured, and pipes lit by the fire, Anneke said, "Will anyone tell me what's going on?"

"The burgher council has voted to increase the defenses of our settlement," Pieter explained. "They mean to put a blockhouse at the junction of the two Indian paths, where it will be easiest for all to reach in time of danger."

"High time," Sytje said. "Mamma and I won't have far to run if it's between our two houses."

"But there's more," Pieter continued. "Several of the councilmen felt our spiritual danger was more pressing than our physical danger and that we should build a church instead. They couldn't agree, so finally they decided to combine the two. The new building at the junction is to be a blockhouse church."

"And Mamma," Jan said, "They've selected me to build it. Pieter stood surety for me."

Anneke jumped up so quickly she knocked over her stool. "My brilliant boy," she said, hugging her son, "I always knew you were meant for great things."

"But a blockhouse church," Sytje said. "I've never heard of such a thing."

"I think it's a wonderful idea," Anneke said. "So much better than building a church inside the fort the way they did in New Amsterdam. That church belonged to the WIC, but this church right in the middle of the settlement will belong to the people. Only I can't quite imagine how it's going to work. What are you thinking, Son?"

"I have so many ideas," Jan said excitedly, "but I want to talk everything over with you. I told the council we shouldn't build a cross-shaped church the way they do back in Europe because that's harder to defend. I want to make it square so men looking out of loopholes can see in all directions."

"Loopholes?" asked Sytje. "Where will they be?"

"I was thinking we might build it on two levels," Jan said. "Women could sit on the ground floor, and then we might have a large balcony running around the upper floor where the men could listen to the sermon and watch for danger at the same time."

"That might work," Pieter said, nodding. "Especially if you place cannons at each of the four corners on the upper story."

In the midst of the excitement about Jan's good fortune, Anneke noticed that Willem seemed subdued, so the next day she asked him to go with her to fetch water from the well.

"What's the matter, Son?" she asked after their heavy buckets had been filled.

"Everyone's so happy for Jan, but what about me? I'll soon be seventeen, but I still have no vocation."

This was a conversation that Anneke had been dreading. More than anything else in the world she wanted to keep Evert's sons away from the church and from politics, but if Willem wanted to follow in his father's footsteps, she had no right to stand in his way.

"You've had more schooling than Jan ever did, and you've always enjoyed it. If you want to go to university, we could ask Pieter or Govert to help send you to Leiden, or if you're not troubled by the English faith, we could send you to Harvard up north."

Willem shook his head. "I don't want to study theology," he said. "I've been staying after school copying legal documents for Meester Adriaen. He says I could earn a good living as a notary, but it would be easier for me to find clients in New Amsterdam."

"Then that's where you should go," Anneke said with relief. "You can stay with your sister until you get a place of your own."

"Thank you, Mother. I knew you'd understand. What about Cornelis?"

"Cornelis?" Anneke stiffened. "Don't tell me *he* wants to study theology."

"No," Willem said, laughing, "he has a different idea. He's been spending time after school with the gunstock makers. Philip Pietersen would like to take him on as an apprentice, but Cornelis is afraid to ask you. He thinks you'll disapprove."

"It's an honorable profession," Anneke said, "and there will always be a need for gunstock makers. I'll go talk to Philip Pietersen, as soon as we get this water stowed."

Femmetje the Baker was undoubtedly awkward, but Anneke remained fond of her. Femmetje had been kind to Anneke during the difficult days after Evert's death, and when Femmetje's husband Hendrick died, Anneke tried to return the kindness.

Hendrick collapsed during the small hours of the morning while treading a trough of *roggebrood.* He was still alive when their thirteen-year-old daughter Grietjen found him. She screamed, and Femmetje and Piet came running. Together they got him into the house, cleaned him off, and got him to bed, where he lingered for several days. When Anneke heard the news, she rushed over, bringing food for the family and taking turns watching over the invalid.

After the burial, she sat with Femmetje, holding her hand and sympathizing, but eventually she posed the inevitable question: "What will you do now?"

"Do? I have to find a husband."

"Femmetje, your bakery stands on a valuable piece of property, and you know everything there is to know about baking. What's to keep you from running the place on your own?"

"I have the knowledge, but I haven't the strength. I can't lift bags of flour. I can't get up in the middle of the night to tread the roggebrood, and then stoke the ovens and keep them the right temperature all day. It's man's work."

"Femmetje, your son Piet can do much of that work, and if he can't do it alone, there are men you could hire. You could take an apprentice. You don't have to marry if you don't want to."

Femmetje shook her head. "I can't afford an apprentice. I have debts."

"Ah," Anneke said, "I understand." And she really did understand. A man might carry large amounts of debt over long periods of time, but the moment he died, creditors would fall on his widow like wolves on a sickly calf.

That evening Anneke told Sytje and Pieter of Femmetje's plight. They sat by the hearth trying to think of anything that might be done.

"Well," Pieter said, "if she's destitute, she can always ask the deacons for help. They might find light work for her, like sewant stringing, or pay her to take in a foster child or a boarder, or give her food and clothing to tide her over."

"It might come to that," Anneke said, "but right now I think she's trying to figure out how to keep the bakery, satisfy her creditors, and feed her family."

"That bakery's right on the water between the first two kills. Would it help if I bought a corner of the lot from her for a new brewery?" Pieter asked.

"It might," Anneke said, "but would you not then be enriching yourself at her expense?"

Pieter shrugged. "I would give her a fair price, and I should think she would rather sell one corner to me than have the entire parcel sold off at auction."

The three hundred guilders Pieter gave Femmetje for her land helped her meet her most pressing obligations, but still she struggled to make ends meet. Govert Loockermans was the first to place a lien on her property, and others soon followed.

After months of flailing about, Femmetje showed up at Anneke's house one frosty November morning with a delivery of fresh bread. She accepted payment in sewant and then smiled shyly at Anneke and said, "I've found a groom."

"Oh my," Anneke said, hiding her dismay. "Tell me about him."

"It's Michiel Anthonisen."

"Michiel?" Anneke asked in open surprise. "I thought he was married."

"He *was* married back in Holland, but he hasn't heard from his wife for five years now, so she must be dead—at least that's what his neighbor says—and he has every right to take a wife. I know people will talk because he's so much younger than me, but I think it's a good thing because baking's too hard for an old man. We've talked it all over. We're going to sell everything here and move to the Kats Kill, and it's all going to be wonderful."

"I hope so," Anneke said. "I really do." She knew as much as the next woman about loneliness, but she still couldn't escape the feeling that Femmetje in desperation was rushing into disaster.

Anneke helped Femmetje dress for her wedding, even putting a crown of spirea on her graying curls. Femmetje had worn herself to a frazzle preparing baked goods for the celebration that followed, but despite the currant buns and barrels of good beer, it seemed to Anneke to be an anxious affair, memorable largely for the misbehavior of Femmetje's teenaged daughter.

Redheaded Grietjen, her face flushed and sweaty and her cap askew, made a spectacle of herself, laughing too loudly at a joke that Tjerck the Carter told and stealing a sip of beer from Jacob the Brewer. She was just about to ask that scapegrace Claes Uylenspiegel to dance with her when Anneke took her firmly by the elbow and led her out into the fresh air.

"Grietjen," Anneke said, "You mustn't spoil your mamma's special day."

"Special day!" Grietjen said angrily. "She's making a fool of herself. Everyone knows she's too old to marry. I had the best pappa in the world, and she can't ever replace him with some stupid Michiel Anthonisen."

"Hush, Grietjen," Anneke said soothingly. "No one wants to replace your pappa, but your mamma's alone now, and she needs help."

By this time, Grietjen was weeping like a child, rubbing her eyes with her grubby fist and wiping her nose on her sleeve.

Grietjen's brother Piet walked up behind them and put his hand on Grietjen's shoulder. "I'll take little sister home," he said to Anneke. "I'll make sure she's all right."

The breaking of the ice on the North River at first sounded like gunfire, but gradually the river cleared enough for travel to resume. The first sloop of the season docked bearing letters, packages, supplies, and passengers. One of the last people to disembark was a woman traveling alone. She appeared to be a person of modest means, but she was neatly dressed, and even though she was clearly fatigued by her long journey, she stepped onto the landing with an air of eager anticipation.

Tjerck the Carter was on hand to pick up a shipment for Volkert Jansen, but he could also take passengers if need be.

"May I assist you, mejuffrouw?" he asked.

"Oh yes, can you please direct me to the home of Michiel Anthonisen?"

"I'm afraid Michiel Anthonisen now lives at the Kats Kill, but we can arrange for you to be taken there tomorrow if you wish. Are you a relative?"

"Oh yes, I most certainly am. I'm Gretchen Jacobs, his wife."

By nightfall, there wasn't a single soul in Beverwyck who didn't know the scandalous story of Michiel Anthonisen and his two wives. The dilemma, according to Pieter, who was both a church elder and a member of the burgher council, was that no one knew whether this unprecedented case should be dealt with by the magistrates or by the church.

"The magistrates, obviously," Anneke said. "Michiel should be fined and forced to make reparations to Femmetje. He has caused her material damage."

"But Mamma," Sytje said, "marriage is sacred. Surely only the church can untangle this mess."

"Then tell me this," Pieter asked. "If I must sit in judgment, which wife should I find for?"

"Femmetje," Anneke said. "Michiel's first wife was silent for five years. That amounts to desertion. Femmetje married him in good faith, and she now has all the rights of his legal wife."

But in the end the burgher council found that Gretchen Jacobs had the prior claim and granted Femmetje a letter of divorce. Their decision was made easier by Femmetje's renouncing her marriage and saying she wanted nothing more to do with Michiel Anthonisen.

Femmetje came to say goodbye to Anneke before leaving for the Esopus. "They told me I was at liberty to marry anyone I like, but I just want to get away from here," she said. "I want to go to a place where no one recognizes me and no one has ever heard of Michiel Anthonisen."

Eleven

WAR ON THE ESOPUS

(1658–1661)

On the Esopus

Sieur Govert Loockermans awakened to the sound of a squalling infant and the smell of horse dung. Under the drowsy impression that the child was his own Jacob, he thought: *Good ol' Marritje. She promised me a son, and*—smiling at his own joke—*by Heaven, she delivered.* Given her age, there probably wouldn't be many more, but a son to carry on his name and two buxom daughters with whom to forge alliances with the other great families were enough for now.

A moment later, Govert jerked wide awake. He was not in his mansion on the strand but on the Esopus at the farmstead of Heer Stuyvesant's tenant farmer, Juriaen Westvael. Heer Stuyvesant had requested that Govert accompany him to investigate the complaints of the settlers there. Light shining through the slats of the stable where Govert had chosen to sleep told him that it was long past dawn, and Heer Stuyvesant, he felt sure, was already up and saddled, ready to start the day.

Govert hurriedly splashed some water on his face and then walked out the back door of the stable so he could casually enter the living portion of the house like a man who had been out reconnoitering since earliest birdsong. To his relief, he found Heer Stuyvesant still finishing his weak beer and discussing the management of the bouwery with Juriaen and his wife Marrichen. The child who had awakened Govert was their newborn, Johannes, quiet now that his mother was nursing him. Two other children, a girl with the odd name Reymerig and her younger brother Claes, sat quietly in the corner staring at their powerful visitor.

"I see that you've already put in barley and oats," Stuyvesant was saying, "but I also want you to get a proper fence up before winter and plant the winter wheat. If you need additional oxen, I can send you some."

Govert slipped into the room as inconspicuously as possible and helped himself to a slab of rye bread.

"And now that Sieur Loockermans has condescended to join us," Stuyvesant continued, "tell us about these grievances we've been receiving. Thom Chambers wrote the letter, but you also put your mark on it, Juriaen. How much of it is true? Are things really so bad here?"

"Things are different here," Juriaen began. "The Dutch up at Beverwyck have good relations with the Wilden because of trade. The River Indians on the Esopus don't have much use for trade, so their young men make mischief. One drunk shot Harmon Jacobsen dead."

"Surely the solution for that problem would be to refrain from selling them alcohol," Stuyvesant said.

"We're not the ones who sell it to them," Marrichen said. "They can get all the brandy they want from Fort Orange."

"And there have been other things," Juriaen continued. "They burned down Jacob Adriaensen's farm."

"Then let's see what we can do to get it all sorted out."

Juriaen saddled two horses and led them to the tree stump that served as a mounting block while Heer Stuyvesant and Govert strapped on swords and pistols and prepared to ride. Their meeting with the villagers would be held midday at the farmstead of Thomas Chambers.

As they rode out from the Westvael Farmstead, Stuyvesant nodded his satisfaction at the fields of wheat and rye in the distance. "It's a fertile land," he said, "worth fighting for."

"I suppose so," said Govert, who was indifferent to crops. "What do you know about Chambers?"

"Not much. He's English, came to Rensselaerswyck as a carpenter, and now seems to be the self-appointed leader of the Esopus settlement. He's smart, ambitious, and ruthless. You'll like him," Stuyvesant said just as the palisaded perimeter of Chambers's farmstead came into view.

Within, they found a dozen or so of the leading men of the community, including Juriaen, who had taken a shortcut through the woods to arrive in advance of his guests. The settlers excitedly voiced their complaints, often repeating things they had already included in their remonstrance, relieved finally to be speaking to the man in charge. And Stuyvesant listened patiently and nodded at each of their grievances, while Govert sharpened a quill and prepared to take notes.

Jacob Jansen, better known as Hap, had lost two pregnant sows, shot just because they were rooting up the savages' crops. "Why can't you make them fence their crops like Christians?" he wanted to know.

"That's nothing," Cornelis Barentsen said. "They made me plow for them. They acted like they were going to set my barn on fire if I didn't."

When each man had been heard, Heer Stuyvesant said, "I see that you have been cruelly used. Tomorrow, Sieur Loockermans and I will meet with the sachems to ascertain guilt and negotiate reparations, but now I must ask each of you how you plan to live moving forward. If the present situation is intolerable, what will you do to change it?"

"The Esopus will never be safe for Christians as long as the River Indians are here," Hap said. "We need you to send troops and clear them all out once and for all so we can farm in peace."

"Alas, that we cannot do. You yourselves must agree that the killing of one man and the burning of a few small houses is insufficient justification for a general declaration of war. And besides, it's almost harvest time. If we go to war, your crops will be ruined, and you will be left destitute and hungry."

"Well then," Cornelis Barentsen said, "If the Wilden must remain, we will continue to live alongside of them, but you must provide troops to protect each of our bouweries."

"Ah! would that we could, but your bouweries are scattered across the landscape like toys on a nursery floor. We could not possibly assign men to each of them."

"What would you have us do then?" Thom Chambers asked.

"Well, you can continue living as you are, unless you have a better idea."

"Such as?" Juriaen asked.

"You might, for example, select some easily fortified location, where you could live together without fear of external enemies. I could order my men to help you build a stockade if you like."

"But that would mean moving our houses!" Cornelis Barentsen objected.

"Your houses were quickly built, and they can be quickly disassembled and put back together again."

"But we each wish to have ready access to the land that we farm," Hap said.

"Then you must decide. Continue as you are without protection, or agree to live together in one protected place."

"I admire your patience, mynheer," Govert said that evening as they rode back to the Westvael Farmstead. "You already know what they need to do. You have the power. Why don't you just tell them?"

"Because, my dear Govert, you can tell a dog what to do, and sometimes it will obey, but settlers are more like cats. You will achieve better results if you persuade them that what you want them to do is their own idea."

By morning the colonists had reached the conclusion that Heer Stuyvesant desired. If the Director General would undertake to assist them in future emergencies, they would pull down their scattered habitations and move close to each other in a fortified place of his choosing.

After the stockade was completed, the settlers had to admit that the location was well chosen. It was virtually inaccessible on three sides but opened on the south to the level plain where they raised their crops. In exchange for the settlers' agreeing to live in a confined location, Stuyvesant also secured a commitment from the Wilden to remove to the interior and leave the Dutch to farm in peace, but just to be on the safe side he left Ensign Dirk Smit and a company of fifty men bivouacked at the Westvael Farmstead.

"You're a grand one for building walls," Govert said to him as they sailed back to New Amsterdam. "First the wall across Manhattan, then Beverwyck, and now this."

"We have been tasked with bringing civilization to this land," Stuyvesant replied. "Civilization means cities, and cities by definition are fortified. While we pray for peace, we must always be prepared to defend what is ours."

Govert returned to the Esopus once more that summer at the request of Heer Stuyvesant to determine whether it was safe for Dirk Smit and his troops to return to New Amsterdam. As before, he stayed at the Westvael Farmstead, choosing to sleep in the stable rather than endure the clamor of the Westvaels' three children.

On his first evening at the farm, he summoned Dirk Smit and asked for his evaluation.

"Well," Smit began, "I guess things are a little better now that most of the settlers have moved into the stockade. People with large areas to farm like Juriaen here or Thomas Chambers decided to stay on their farms, but they get along fairly well with the Wilden. Chambers even hires them as day laborers . . ."

Even as he was finishing his sentence, they heard gunfire coming from the stockade.

Smit and Govert rushed for their horses—Smit shouting commands for ten of his men to follow them—and galloped toward the stockade. They arrived to a scene of turmoil just outside the stockade gates. One Indian lay dead on the ground, and a very drunk Hap was putting a rope around the neck of another Indian so drunk he could scarcely stand.

Smit slid from his saddle and rushed to remove the rope from the Indian's neck. "Let's get this boy to the guardhouse," he said, "and you come, too, Hap. You've got some explaining to do."

Hap was incapable of coherent explanation, but Cornelis Barentsen was happy to fill in the gaps. The problem started, he said, earlier that evening when Thomas Chambers gave a group of eight Indian day laborers an anker of brandy for helping him bring in the maize.

"Was he trying to start a war!" Govert exclaimed. "All of you know that it is expressly forbidden to provide the Natives with alcohol."

Cornelis Barentsen shrugged. "Maybe that was all he had on hand. Anyway, the eight of them started partying right outside the stockade, and their whooping and yelling was making the rest of us on the inside nervous. Hap just couldn't stand the noise anymore, so he yelled, 'By Heaven, I'll put a bit in their mouth. All Christians follow me!' and about seven of us grabbed our weapons and ran after him. We just meant to chase the Wilden away, but one boy got himself shot dead by accident, and another one was too drunk to run, so we had to take him captive."

"By Christ's suffering wounds!" Smit swore the following morning. "I ought to take my men back to Fort Amsterdam and leave those pigheaded settlers to stew in their own juices."

"It's tempting," Govert said, "but you'd best wait for orders from Stuyvesant."

"True," Smit said with a sigh. "I don't suppose you'd like to carry a message to him."

"I'd *love* to," Govert replied, "but I have a feeling he would want me to stay here. Pick two other men and send them on that sloop that's about to depart, and then we'll see what his instructions are."

Messengers were chosen, and a group of soldiers and settlers accompanied them to the landing. Relieved that the messengers had safely departed, the escort group was making its way slowly back up the hill to the stockade when the Indians struck. Hap was mortally wounded, which some uncharitable souls regarded as divine retribution, and numerous others, including Thomas Chambers, were taken captive.

Toward evening on the same day, a group of Indians bearing a white flag approached the stockade. Chambers had talked them into exchanging him for their own lad who was still being held in the guardhouse. They wanted ransom for the others.

The siege began the following day. The fighting was not constant, but the threat was always there. No one but soldiers were permitted to leave the enclosure, so the settlers' fine crops—the best they'd had in years—rotted in the field. Outlying buildings were burned, and they could hear their livestock crying first from hunger and then as they were slaughtered. Men and the older boys stood watch with loaded weapons and shot at anything that moved while women and children prepared buckets of water to douse burning arrows.

Govert rode through the streets of the settlement surveying the damage and encouraging the men on watch. He bitterly regretted his decision not to return to New Amsterdam with the messengers. Ahead of him, he saw a gray-haired woman sitting on the stoop outside of the bakery with her face buried in her apron. Beside her, a pudgy teenager with unruly strands of red hair poking out from under her cap seemed to be cajoling the woman or perhaps attempting to comfort her. The woman lifted her head, and Govert recognized her as Femmetje the Baker, a person who owed him money. The teenager was undoubtedly her bratty daughter Grietjen.

"Hoi, Baker!" Govert hailed Femmetje. "Why aren't you working? There are hungry mouths to be fed."

"How dare you speak to my mother like that!" Grietjen shouted, leaping to her feet. "Haven't we enough troubles without the likes of you around?"

Govert really wanted to strike the child, but he realized that a spat with a teenaged girl would reflect poorly on him, so he said in a quieter voice, "I ask you again, woman. Why aren't you working?"

"My son . . . my Piet . . . taken away," Femmetje said, weeping.

"Well, that's no problem," Govert said with a confidence he didn't feel. "We'll pay the ransom and get him back for you in no time. But look here! You've let your oven go cold."

"That was Piet's job!"

Govert sighed and dismounted. "Well, we can't have that, now can we? Grietjen, come help me get the oven lighted again, and then the two of you will bake some bread. Bread and beer are the staves of life, heh? People depend on you, and you mustn't let them down."

Beverwyck

Anneke and a group of other women were whitewashing the interior of the blockhouse church when Jan ran in with news of the catastrophe on the Esopus. "Come quickly to the fort," he called to them. "The Esopus settlers are under siege."

As they all entered the fort, they could hear Commissary La Montagne addressing the sixty-some people assembled before him. "Fort Orange and Beverwyck are in no immediate danger," he assured them, "but we have been charged with recruiting men to join the relief force and with raising ransom funds. I will also need to ask some of you to open your homes and provide shelter for the refugees."

"How do you know we're in no danger?" Tjerck the Carter shouted. "What are you doing to protect us?"

"At the request of the community," La Montagne said, gesturing to the crowd before him, "we have instituted a rattle watch to patrol between the hours of ten o'clock and four o'clock."

"Two men with a wooden rattle might alert us to fires or thieves, but they can't do much to protect us from Wilden," Jacob the Brewer protested. "What are you doing about them?"

"Tomorrow, I and all of the members of your burgher council past and present will meet with a delegation of Mohawks here at the fort. They do not want this disruption any more than we do and will act as intermediaries if need be. We have also been directed to create a place for trade with the Wilden outside of the town walls. No Indians will be permitted to enter Beverwyck until this crisis has been resolved."

"There goes my livelihood," Anneke muttered to Jan.

On the Esopus

The siege continued throughout the fall. Messengers came and messengers went as intermediaries tried to negotiate a truce. The men of Fort Orange scurried to raise additional ransom funds, and Petrus Stuyvesant at Fort Amsterdam scrambled to raise relief troops. At last he resorted to instituting a draft and by that means was finally able to bring a force of about two hundred men, both professionals and draftees along with a number of Long Island Indians, to relieve the besieged village. The draftees were rubbish, of course, but at least they made a great noise and created the appearance of a substantial army.

The Esopus Indians, who knew exactly where Stuyvesant was and how many men he had, vanished into the interior on the eve of his arrival. The siege was over, but the war had just begun.

Ensign Smit received instructions from Stuyvesant to wait until spring and then take captives. In March, he did just that. He and his men came across a group of about sixty Esopus Indians—mostly women and children guarded by a few young men—putting in crops some three miles distant from the settlement. Many escaped, but fifteen were captured and sent to Fort Amsterdam. Heer Stuyvesant, thinking to project strength and inspire fear, sent ten of the captives into slavery in Curaçao. The remainder he retained as pawns to be exchanged for European prisoners.

Smit and his troops continued their military offensive. They slogged through the sodden spring woods at the pace of snails. They espied an Indian stockade on the other side of Esopus Creek, but the stream was too swollen for them to cross. They returned in failure to the Westvael Farmstead, where Marrichen explained to them where the ford was located.

The following day, following Marrichen's directions, they came to a fortified Indian village. They made too much noise to surprise anyone, but the elderly Sachem Premaeker remained to confront them. He said, "What are you doing here, you dogs?" so they whacked him on the head with his own hatchet. Then they destroyed habitations and food stores and returned to the settlement with their plunder.

By the following July, all parties were exhausted. Prisoners were exchanged, and a permanent and lasting treaty of peace and friendship was signed on the Esopus under the blue sky of Heaven. To compensate the Dutch for their troubles, all of the land on both sides of Esopus Creek would be ceded to them, and in honor of the Esopus Indians who were making such a generous donation, the settlement would henceforth be known as Wiltwyck.

Beverwyck

To celebrate the coming of peace, Petrus Stuyvesant ordered a Day of Thanksgiving throughout New Netherland. Anneke attended the service at the blockhouse church and fervently prayed in her heart, "Thank You, Lord God, for bringing an end to this senseless war. I beg You to have mercy on the souls of those who have died, and I thank You for the lives that You saw fit to spare and for restoring Femmetje's son Piet to his mother. That poor woman has suffered enough. And please, Lord," she added as an afterthought, "please let normal trade resume." And even as she prayed, she thought: *Surely our small settlements by the water can do the Wilden no harm. Surely this war with them must be the last.*

REMEMBER ME

(1661–1663)

Beverwyck

When it became safe to travel again, Sytje received a packet of letters from Sara, some of them written before the outbreak of hostilities more than a year ago. Anneke nodded with satisfaction when she learned Sara had named her baby boy Jochem in honor of her husband's late brother, and she laughed when Sytje read to her that Hans and some of his fellow barber-surgeons had petitioned the burgher council to outlaw the unseemly behavior of the unlicensed riffraff who undermine the entire profession by lying in wait for incoming ships and shaving all and sundry at ridiculously low prices. The council had rejected the petition, decreeing that barbering was but a secondary part of a surgeon's profession and therefore could not be regulated.

"What was he thinking?" she cried, wiping away tears of laughter. "It's a free country. People can have their faces shaved by anyone they like, and if they get their throats cut, all the more work for the surgeons."

In one early letter, Sara described Willem's arrival in New Amsterdam. "Dearest Mother and Sister," she wrote, "You will be pleased to learn our brother Willem has been successful in attracting new clients and soon will be moving into lodgings of his own, despite our protests, for he is dear to us and we are in no hurry to part with him. Hans is of the opinion that peering closely at legal documents is putting unnecessary strain on his eyes, so he has ordered a pair of spectacles for him from Holland. I will let you know when they arrive and how our brother takes to them." Then in a later letter she wrote that her shy and scholarly brother had begun keeping company with the notoriously light-minded Wyntje Sybrands. The couple had already posted banns, and unless Sara was very much mistaken, Wyntje was already with child.

And late July brought another welcome visit from Marritje, who arrived with trunk loads of gifts.

"I know, I know," she said to Anneke, pulling out coifs and aprons, neckerchiefs and napkins, silk hoods for Anneke and Sytje, *kolf* sticks and tin telescopes for her nephews, and a small ivory tobacco box for Pieter, "It probably looks like I've come to set up shop, but life is just too short not to spoil my nearest and dearest."

"I've missed you," Anneke said, setting out fresh cider and stewed pork. "I'm truly glad you've come, but where's Jacob? I wanted to meet him."

"I left him with Elsie. She has four of her own now, you know, and Jacob is the same age as her oldest, so he's happier at her house, and Govert's daughters still resent him, so I try to keep him out of their way as much as I can."

"How are you getting along with Lysbet Setten these days?"

"Much better now that she's dead. Maryken and Janneken have accepted me if not as a mother then at least as an ally—especially now that they've become interested in boys, and I've found the most extraordinary way to keep them home and out of trouble. I can't wait to tell you."

"You'll have to wait," Anneke said, laughing. "I want to hear about my own children first. Did Willem really marry Wyntje Sybrands? Sara said she thought the girl was pregnant."

"She was, and he did. I never believed the child was Willem's, but clearly he did because when they had the boy baptized three months after the wedding, Willem named him Everardus . . ."

Anneke gasped and bit the knuckle of her hand.

". . . but the poor mite didn't live long. Probably for the best, but I'm sorry to bring you sad news, Sister," Marritje said, squeezing Anneke's hand. "I thought you already knew."

When Anneke awakened shortly after dawn the following morning, she found her indefatigable sister out in the chicken coop collecting eggs.

"Oh good, you're up," Marritje said. "I have the most amazing thing to show you."

Back at the house, Marritje plunged once more into her trunk and emerged with an iron contraption that consisted of a perforated barrel turned by a handle suspended over a shallow tray. "This was Govert's wedding present to me," she said.

"How romantic," Anneke said.

"Yeah, I was furious until I found the diamond brooch hidden inside. But Govert was right. This thing is more valuable than diamonds. It entertains me, provides me with pocket money, and helps me keep the peace with Maryken and Janneken. It's called a roaster, and this is what we're going to roast," she said producing a small bag of pale green beans.

"They look like gray peas," Anneke said. "Wouldn't it be better to boil them?"

"These are the pits of coffee cherries, and they come from Java. Look, I'm going to put some coals in the bottom tray of my roaster, put the coffee seeds into the barrel, and turn the handle until the seeds turn brown, and while I'm doing that, I want you to boil a pan of spring water until it's reduced by about a half."

About an hour later, Marritje poured her roasted pits into Anneke's mortar and ground them to a coarse powder. "Now," she said, "we'll add the coffee powder and a little sugar to your spring water, and let it boil gently for another forty-five minutes until it turns into coffee wine."

"I can certainly see how anything so complicated keeps you occupied, but what does it have to do with Maryken and Janneken?" Anneke asked.

"Men pay good money for coffee wine," Marritje answered. "Other women serve beer and wine and spirits in their front parlors, and I've taken to selling coffee."

"How can you manage to make coffee every day when it takes so long to prepare?" Anneke asked.

"Anneke," Marritje said gently, "we have servants. I have a scullery maid who roasts the pits and prepares the beverage. She keeps a pot of it warm by the fire and serves it to our paying guests. The leading men of the community come to my house for conversation and coffee, and many of the younger ones as well. And on the afternoons when we serve coffee, Maryken and Janneken delight in playing hostess. For them, it's an opportunity to dress in ribbons and lace and to meet handsome young men whom they would normally see only at church. Stuyvesant's nephews are regulars, and one of our most frequent guests is your grandson Hansel."

Marritje spent the rest of the summer with Anneke in Beverwyck, cooking and cleaning, attending services, and teaching Sytje's daughters nonsense verse that made them all laugh.

"Next year," she said, as she was preparing to leave, "I want you all to come and stay with me. Pieter can go about his business, Sytje's girls can get to know their cousins, and you and I, Anneke, can visit the new Indian trading market they built last year in front of Sara's house. It's just amazing to watch that girl jibber-jabber with the Natives in their own tongue. You must be so proud of her."

"I'm proud of all of my children," Anneke said.

"Oh, and there's one other thing I wanted to ask you about before I leave. Govert was wondering whether you might be interested in selling him those two houses you own in New Amsterdam. He was thinking you might be able to use some extra money to help your youngest two get started in life."

As was the custom, Anneke attended both of Sytje's earlier births, and she was also present at the last one when the midwife said, "The baby's turned the wrong way. I can't get it out. If you send for a surgeon, maybe he can cut the child out and save the mother, or cut the mother and save the child."

Pieter had refused. "Let God's Will be done," he said, "but I will not have her cut."

Everyone left then except for Pieter and Anneke, and together they waited as Anneke lost her daughter, and Pieter lost the love of his life and his whole reason for living.

When it was over, Anneke tended her daughter's body while Pieter went to the church to rent the pall for her burial. Then Anneke took her granddaughters, Jannetje and Rachel, back to her house and told them they would be living with her for a time.

Rachel cried for her mamma, and Jannetje cried for her pappa, but Anneke told them their mamma was looking over them from Heaven and their pappa had things he needed to do on Manhattan, but he loved them so.

"And look," she said to the weeping children, "I think we need something special for supper today. How about we all make some waffles?"

Pieter remained in New Amsterdam for over a year. Anneke had been certain he would remarry there and then send for his girls, but as time passed with no word from him, she began to think of Jannetje and Rachel as her own. She sewed skirts and capes for them, taught them to knit and to darn, and sent them to school, as she had done her own daughters, so at least they could learn to read. Of an evening, she taught them to say their prayers, praising God for His Wisdom, entreating Him to have mercy on their mamma and to protect their pappa, who was far away. And as she prayed with them, she thought to herself: *Truly God moves in mysterious ways. He has taken my daughters from me but given me these two glorious girls to brighten my days.*

When Pieter finally did return to Beverwyck, he seemed troubled, and after the girls had gone to bed, he told Anneke he needed to talk to her.

"Don't be shy about telling me you've found yourself a new woman," she said. "I understand man is meant to live in matrimony."

"It's not that," Pieter said. "New Netherland has become hateful to me, and I take no joy in the things that once pleased me. I've come to Beverwyck to sell all of my property here, and when all of those transactions have been completed, I mean to return to Patria."

"And the girls?" Anneke asked, holding her breath.

"The girls will come with me. In my grief, I've neglected them, but that is going to change now. We will live together as God intends, as a family."

On the day Pieter left Beverwyck to return to Patria, he brought Jannetje and Rachel to say goodbye to their *oma*. Anneke was dry-eyed and heartbroken. She had raised these girls, and they were all she had left of Sytje. She would not criticize their father's decision, but he sensed her distress and tried to explain once again why he wanted his daughters to live in Europe.

"The girls need a stepmother. Don't tell me there's any woman in the colony you think would be good enough for them."

Anneke shook her head. "No."

"And in Amsterdam they will have access to the highest reaches of society. Besides, I know it's what Sytje would have wanted. We always talked about moving to Patria, but she wanted to wait . . ."

Until I was dead, Anneke thought.

" . . . until the new baby was strong enough to travel. She didn't want her children to grow up thinking slavery was normal."

Anneke was taken aback. *Was slavery becoming normal?* Govert bought a manservant last year, but he only did it to be fashionable. It was true that last month there had been a public auction of a man, a woman, and two children in Beverwyck, but it was hard to imagine such a thing ever happening again.

The next morning she went to the landing to say her farewells. She handed each of her granddaughters a handkerchief edged in black and told them, "Remember me, remember your mother."

Then she turned and walked slowly back to her home at the junction.

A great many people were in town today—Wilden and Swanneken alike. Perhaps she might be able to trade for some maize meal or some dried pumpkin. She would have loved to have some venison jerky, but she didn't have the teeth for it anymore. Ahead of her in the crowd she saw the familiar silhouette of a slender woman with a long braid. Without thinking, she cried out, "Ichu! My friend!"

The stranger turned and looked at her with incomprehension. Anneke covered her eyes with her hand and shook her head in apology, "I'm so sorry, my mistake, my error."

What was she thinking? Welanie would be a grandmother by now . . . or a great-grandmother . . . or dead.

As a young woman Anneke had chafed at the notion of predestination. "If God intends for me to be damned for all eternity," she complained to Evert, "why did He even bother to put me in this world in the first place?"

"I don't think God intends for anyone to be damned," Evert said, "but He knows in advance the choices we will make."

"But how are we supposed to know which choices lead to salvation?" Anneke argued. "We need some sort of method. If we had a clear set of rules, all of us would follow them, and no one would ever go to Hell."

How foolish she had been, how naive to think that she could have made all the right choices even if she had known the rules! When she thought back over her life and especially over the thirty years she had spent in the colony, she realized how few of the things that mattered the most—her coming to this land, her two marriages, the ten children she had borne and the three she had buried—had depended on her own volition. And it was a comfort now to think that her many mistakes—both large and small and even the ones she didn't know she had made—no longer mattered because

God had always known the outcome, and soon enough so would she.

"Son," she called to Jonas who was lugging heavy sacks of grain to the upstairs loft, "run and fetch me a notary. I want to write my will."

Epilogue

THE WILL OF ANNEKE JANS

(1663)

The will of Anneke Jans, written in 1663, was entirely unremarkable for the time in which it was written. As was the custom, Anneke requested that all of her property be divided equally among her eight children, with Sytje's daughters Jannetje and Rachel receiving their mother's portion. Before any distribution could be made, she specified that Roelof's children should receive the one thousand guilders that was still owed to them from their father's estate, and that each of her unmarried children should receive a mattress and a milch cow, which, she said, was the equivalent of what she had given their married siblings. She also requested that silver memory cups be made for Sytje's daughters and for three of her other grandchildren named for people she had lost: Sara's son Roelof, Katryn's daughter Anna, and Willem's daughter Sytje.

The trouble began a decade later when her heirs, with the exception of son Cornelis, who had died, sold Roelof's

Farm (Dominee's Bouwery) to the Colonial Governor of New York, Francis Lovelace. When Lovelace was recalled, his New World holdings became property of the Crown. In 1705, Queen Anne bestowed the land on Trinity Church. *Much* later (around 1830), a descendant of Cornelis initiated proceedings to recover the portion of the property that he claimed still belonged to his branch of the family. Other lawsuits followed well into the twentieth century making the case of Anneke Jans's Farm one of the longest and most notorious property wrangles in the history of New York.

SOURCES

Anneke Jans in the New World, although a work of fiction, is based on real events that took place in New Netherland. In a few instances quotations from published translations of Dutch documents have been incorporated in the novel. *Council Minutes, 1638–1649* can be found on the Website of the New Netherland Institute.

Chapter Five

Kieft's charge to the Twelve Men: *Council Minutes, 1638–1649*, trans. Arnold J. F. van Laer. New York Historical Manuscripts: Dutch (Baltimore, 1974), 124.

Chapter Six

Kieft's justification: *Council Minutes, 1638–1649*, 187.
Remonstrance of the Eight Men: *Documents Relative to the Colonial History of the State of New York*, ed. E. B. O'Callaghan (Albany, 1856), 1: 213.

Chapter Seven

Evert's Sermon: *Council Minutes, 1638–1649*, 295–296.
Stuyvesant's instructions: *Council Minutes, 1638–1649*, 370.

Chapter Eight

Kieft's apology: *Broad Advice to the United Netherland Provinces*, trans. Henry C. Murphy (New York, 1857), 267.

Chapter Nine

Govert's correspondence: "Govert Loockermans Correspondence," trans Wim Vanraes for the New Netherland Institute (2014), 45, 54.

ACKNOWLEDGMENTS

Above all, I would like to thank the many translators who have labored to make Dutch archival records available in English. I am also grateful for the resources made available by the New Netherland Institute, the New Amsterdam History Center, the Jacob Leisler Institute, and the Holland Society of New York.

I have benefited from the scholarship of Mary C. Beaudry, David Vernooy Bennett, William Bogardus, Andrew Brink, Anne-Marie Cantwell, Bernard Capp, Jeroen Dewulf, Toya Dubin, Firth Haring Fabend, Marc B. Fried, Willem Frijhoff, Andrea E. Frohne, Charles T. Gehring, Joyce D. Goodfriend, Deborah Hamer, Paul R. Huey, Jaap Jacobs, Meta F. Janowitz, Nicole Saffold Maskiell, Donna Merwick, Andrea C. Mosterman, David E. Narrett, Jerome R. Reich, Oliver A. Rink, Robert C. Ritchie, Susanah Shaw Romney, Peter G. Rose, Eric W. Sanderson, Marius Schoonmaker, Russell Shorto, L. F. Tantillo, Janny Venema, David William Voorhees, Diana diZerega Wall, and Henri and Barbara van der Zee, among others. Needless to say, all misinterpretations and errors are entirely my own.

Many thanks also go to book coach Michele Orwin and to Brooke Warner, Megan Milton, Sheila Trask, and Ann Marie Jackson of She Writes Press for their expertise and support.

ABOUT THE AUTHOR

Author photo © Studio Nagila Photography

Sandra Freels majored in Russian at Indiana University and completed a PhD in Slavic Languages and Literatures at Stanford University. The author of three textbooks, for many years she headed the Russian program at Portland State University.

An interest in genealogy led Sandra to the Council Records of New Netherland and the delicious stories of the people who once lived there. She claims descent from Anneke Jans and sixteen other major and minor characters in *Anneke Jans in the New World.*

At present, Sandra lives with her husband Joel and their two cats in Portland, Oregon.

Thank you for reading *Anneke Jans in the New World.*
For more information about Anneke and
suggested discussion questions,
please visit www.sandrafreels.com.